HEART OF STONE

FAMILY STONE #3 RILEY

LISA HUGHEY

January 2014

Lisa Hughey

Ebook ISBN: 978-0-9840428-8-3

Print ISBN: 978-0-9991951-7-8

Cover Artwork – © 2018 L.J. Anderson of Mayhem Cover Creations

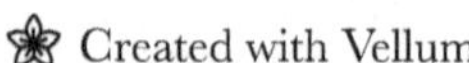 Created with Vellum

ONE

*wo weeks earlier*

RILEY STONE DIDN'T HAVE a *type*.

He loved all women equally. Short, Tall, Skinny, Round. Outgoing. Shy. Young. Old. Sweet. Sexy. Surly.

And they loved him right back.

When he was younger, he'd come to the very happy conclusion, that he could charm his way out of, or sometimes into, any touchy situation.

He'd developed the skill as a young kid. When he'd realized that he was never going to be a good reader, or a good student, he'd made the decision that he'd have to rely on his other attributes. He could charm his grades up from any teacher in whose class he might need a little help. Which came in handy when he knew he wasn't going to pass a test.

He made it a point to always have something nice to say.

As an adult, charming people was second nature. He didn't even have to think about doing it.

When he grew up, he finally understood that his talent was in making people feel better about themselves and better in general. How he approached a situation might vary from person to person, and if using a little charm eased the way, he was gonna use it.

He was shallow enough to use his God given talent to charm women into bed, at least he had been. These days he was more focused on making a go of GHR and Stone Consulting with his brothers and sister than in scoring with a hot woman.

But he still couldn't help himself when it came to charming people, especially women.

"How's it going, sweetheart?" He stopped to chat with Ava Sanchez, his brother Jack's assistant, making her blush and stammer. She was a complete hottie and didn't even seem to realize it. But Riley's Rules Number Ten: Never do more than lightly flirt with co-workers.

He'd managed to maintain an amicable relationship with every woman he'd ever had a thing with. It was a particular point of pride with him. But odds were, at some time, things wouldn't end well. And he'd never jeopardize a working relationship, or Global Humanitarian Relief and Stone Consulting, which meant sweet Ava was off limits.

He smiled gently at her. "He ready for me?"

"Yes. You can go on in," she replied with a tilt of her head. "He's got company."

"Client?"

She nodded, lowered her lashes and smiled.

"Okay." Riley paused to adjust the cuffs of his Egyptian cotton dress shirt and smooth his hand down his bright geometric Jhane Barnes tie. He made it a point to be well-dressed in the office in case there were meetings with clients. It was rare but it did happen. From his vantage point in the doorway, he could see there was a woman in Jack's office. He didn't recognize her from the back. She seemed delicate, the curve of her head covered with a riot of short blond curls and her body language screamed supreme annoyance.

Riley curved his lips into a casual smile and sauntered into Jack's office. His big gruff brother seemed to be conversing carefully with the woman across from him.

Jack looked up and the hard set of his shoulders relaxed. "Ry, you're here." A desperate smile lit his face as he stood and grabbed Riley's hand like a lifeline. "I'd like you to meet, Diana Lundberg from *Tools for Schools*."

The woman stood abruptly and shoved out her hand in a very masculine move to greet him.

She was tall, more sleek lines and hard angles, than soft curves but when her firm, capable fingers curled around his much larger palm, Riley took a serious punch to the gut. Lust hit, hard and unexpected, as he grasped her far more delicate fingers and gazed into her wary, pale blue eyes.

"Pleasure," he finally murmured dazedly.

She tugged her hand from his and turned to Jack. "*He's* going to take TFS into the jungle?" Her curved brow was derisive and her tone bordered on insolent.

Jack leapt to Riley's defense. "He's extremely well-trained and has knowledge of the area."

"I'm a lot more adaptable than I look." Riley smiled seductively, unable to stop the flow of innuendo. He wanted her. Bad. He carefully put his hands in his pockets to stop the instinctive need to reach out and grab her hand again. He hated to do it as it ruined the line of his fine wool gabardine trousers but desperate times and desperate measures. It wouldn't do to accost the client.

She snorted. "I'm sure."

Her abrasive attitude was starting to drill into the haze of attraction he was lost in. "Where am I headed?"

"Philippines," Jack clipped out. "Jolo Island, specifically."

Great. He'd had plenty of experience in country. Not his favorite as the political climate sucked almost as bad as the weather this time of year. Monsoon season was just about over, but the weather didn't always conform to the timetables put out by man. Not to mention the bugs. He shuddered. But he would deal. "Cargo?"

"School supplies," Jack replied.

"Piece of cake." Riley grinned, exposed his white teeth and tried to put her at ease. But he got lost in the magnetism she exuded like a force field even as he noted peripherally the angry vibe that radiated from her.

But angry babe wasn't put at ease. If anything, she stiffened even further while her pale eyes shot sparks at him. "*I* am going to the Philippines. I am not so sure about you."

But Riley had stopped listening at *I*.

"Wait, what?" His eyebrows rose and he snapped his head toward Jack. He straightened from his nonchalant slouch and snatched his hands from his pockets. "You can't possibly expect me to take her," he gestured, careful to keep his voice low-key and well-modulated. "To Jolo Island."

A rosy flush of annoyance spread across her high delicate cheekbones as she pursed her pale pink lips and her body vibrated with a fine tension.

"Exactly," Di said. She dismissed Riley with a disdainful sweep of her lashes and trained her gaze on Jack. "Who else do you have?"

While he was insulted by the rejection , he was more concerned about her intention to travel to the Philippines, Jolo Island specifically. "You don't want to go there." Riley

was shaking his head and trying to figure her out her. "You can't."

"I absolutely can. And I absolutely will."

"Look, sweetheart—"

"My name is Diana," she gritted out between clenched teeth. "Please use it."

"Okay, Di," Riley tried his super-patented, guaranteed to make the toughest critic crack, smile. "You are talking about an area overrun with pirates and terrorists, the MNLF has been entrenched there for years, and general citizens are trying to stay out of everyone's way and just survive. It's no place for a woman of your "

"Are you kidding me?" she snarled. "It's my company. Of course I'm going."

Riley blinked. Why wasn't she listening to him? "It's not safe."

"I know. That's why we're delivering the supplies personally," Di ground out.

"It's not safe for *you*," Riley argued.

She patiently crossed her arms over her chest and drew Riley's gaze to the small, perfectly plump handfuls, covered and lovingly cupped by the ice blue crew neck Henley. "That's why I hired GHR."

"Schools get destroyed with disconcerting frequency there." Riley communicated the information with a pang. Kids needed all the help they could get.

"Again, that's why I hired Jack."

But she hadn't hired Jack, she'd hired GHR. And Riley was truly the best choice for this particular job. He thought about the kids and school supplies and the books they needed. For more reasons than one, he would make sure that they got their supplies. Alone.

"Tools for Schools hired GHR," Jack interjected firmly.

He glanced between the two combatants, and a smug smile quirked his mouth. "And Riley is the most qualified employee for this drop."

Diana stalked toward the door. "We'll discuss this again. I'll send the manifests and weight load next week." She looked like she wanted to slam the door shut but instead she stiffened her shoulders, and swept from the office like a Southern belle in full, hoop-skirted regalia.

Riley just stared after her, admiring the subtle sway of her ass in her tight jeans as she walked out the door.

"What just happened ?" Riley asked bewilderedly. He couldn't wrap his mind around her animosity, especially in the face of his overwhelming lust.

"You just got shut down." Jack shouted with laughter. He bent over, shoulders shaking, hand to his stomach, as if he couldn't contain himself any more. "You finally found a woman immune to your charm."

 *resent day*

DI PACED BACK and forth at the gate. She'd gotten through security in record time for which she was grateful. In the past two weeks, she had tried to convince Jack Stone, repeatedly, to send someone else, someone who didn't care that she was going along on this trip, someone who wasn't Riley Stone. *Anyone* who wasn't Riley Stone, in fact.

Even Jack had attempted to dissuade her from traveling with GHR to deliver the school supplies. And Riley Stone had continued to batter her, via the phone, about not going to Jolo, and staying home to let him make the delivery.

They'd had multiple...discussions with each growing more contentious. Fortunately since she ran Tools for Schools, she wasn't backing down. What he didn't understand was that she had to go with him. Her contacts would only deal with her. The residents of Jolo were distrustful of strangers. They wouldn't accept his presence, or anyone else's for that matter, without her.

If GHR hadn't come so highly recommended by her friends Lailani and Magtanggol, and if she'd been able to find another company on short notice, she'd have dumped them. But she was stuck if she wanted to get the books and paper and instructional supplies delivered on time. The kids were counting on her and TFS to get them the tools they needed to succeed. The only way to break the cycle of poverty that permeated the culture was to educate the kids, especially the girls. And Di refused to let her friends down.

Not to mention the fact that GHR was footing the bill for the transport and delivery of all the supplies. The Global Humanitarian Relief was funded by donations and a good portion of the Stone fortune. With the money that she was saving on shipping she could afford to supply additional schools. It had been hard enough to choose which schools would benefit now and which ones would have to wait until her next trip.

But Riley Freaking Stone didn't seem to want to listen to her. Jeez, the man pushed all her buttons.

She knew his type. All glitz, no substance. He wouldn't even look twice at someone like her. She didn't wear short skirts, stilettos, or a double D bra. She wore jeans, motorcycle boots, and her breasts barely made bumps in her simple cotton shirts.

She didn't drink fancy martinis. She was strictly a beer girl. She didn't slather on makeup. She slapped on moisturizer and maybe a little lip gloss because otherwise her lips chapped. And—

What the hell was she thinking? Di reined in her temper which had started to boil and her imagination which had supplied a very detailed, specific picture of Riley Stone out for drinks with a beauty queen chick wrapped around his gorgeous frame.

She didn't need Riley Stone to go out with her. She just needed him to help her deliver the school supplies that she'd sweated blood and tears to collect, to help the school children in the most ravaged areas, torn apart by political instability, greed, and the random destruction caused by the fighting between the Moro National Liberation Front, various other rebels, and the government.

That's what Riley and Jack didn't understand. She really wasn't trying to be difficult. She *had* to go. The contacts for Tools for Schools were hers. And they were slow to trust. Slow to believe in good, their lives a constant barrage of bad. Now was the right time. The country's government and MNLF and other rebels had a cemented a peace accord in July, and the political climate was perfect for a humanitarian mission. She wasn't stupid. She did understand there were dangers.

But what they didn't understand was her compulsion to help those who had helped raise her. She had an obligation to give back to the community that supported her and nurtured her when she was growing up.

Everyone hoped that the accord would hold and the government and rebels could work out their differences. But that hope was tempered by the reality that the two factions had been fighting for years. There was tentative promise that the region was finally on the road to peace. But that road was littered with past optimism and past disappointment.

She prayed Riley wouldn't leave her in Jolo when he discovered that she'd left the most important, and most difficult to access, school off the official itinerary. Her childhood friend, Lailani, ran the school and her daughter

Divina was the most needy recipient of Di's donations. It was located in a remote area with a fairly treacherous trek to get there. And housed the largest concentration of MNLF rebels on island so the place was still considered fairly hostile at least by the U.S. government.

Di headed for the coffee kiosk in the International terminal at San Francisco International Airport. The Monterey Regional Airport didn't have international flight capabilities or runway length for the large cargo plane, so they'd had to travel to San Francisco. The good news was they could fly straight from San Francisco to Jolo Island in the Sulu Archipelago.

She'd barely slept last night, worrying about all the obstacles that they'd face. And worrying about Riley Stone and her unwilling and annoying attraction to him. She knew he was a player and had no loyalty to any woman. Guys like him were bad news.

Unfortunately, her body wasn't getting the message. Her brain knew but her hormones didn't care. Because she was unduly attracted to him. And why the hell was she dwelling on Riley Stone?

Dammit. She needed caffeine. Bad.

Guys like him thrived on the conquest, whether he had any interest in the spoils or not. She refused to let him see that she was not immune to his personal brand of sexy. Even though, damn, he was unbelievably hot.

But he knew it. And that was the biggest turn off of all. She refused to reveal that she held anything but disdain for him and his slick moves. She hated to admit that his confidence was just as attractive as his body. But the last thing she needed was sex with an over-confident stud like Riley Stone.

That was that.

Riley strode through the crowded cargo terminal, his duffel slung across one shoulder. The security checkpoint had been a bitch. Even with his "permission to carry" on board the plane and bring into a foreign country, he'd been drilled about his weapons and intentions. What he planned to do while he was there, how long he'd be there, and where exactly he'd be going.

If he'd gotten more than a few hours sleep it would have helped but every time he closed his eyes he saw Di's pale blue eyes flashing, her x-rated mouth pursed, her pert breasts bouncing, and the lean line of her torso as she stormed out of Jack's office a few weeks ago, which was the last time he'd seen her in person.

They'd had plenty of conversations over the phone.

She couldn't stand him. Which honestly confused Riley. Everyone liked him.

He'd never met a person he couldn't charm, but Diana Lundberg seemed to be the exception.

And if Di knew, that in addition to his job to deliver school supplies, he had a mission to gather as much intelligence on the political climate in the midst of the peace accord, to document the location of any MNLF camps he ran into, the true attitude of the government toward the peace accord, even the true position of the MNLF, she would gut him with his own K-Bar.

Publicly the government was very pleased with the cessation of violence treaty and open to finding a peaceful solution to years of strife, violence and confrontation. But there was a general feeling in the U.S. that perhaps privately the Philippine government was less receptive to the terrorist peace accord than they had publicly declared. In the past, the Philippine government felt that if they gave in and negotiated with the MNLF it would weaken their effectiveness overall. However, the hope was that the political climate really was shifting toward peace.

Unfortunately, intelligence reports suggested the latest thwarted bomb plot in Manila had originated in the Sulu Province. And again, that could be from a very small, disgruntled faction of the rebels, but the details regarding who instigated the plot were still sketchy.

All they really had right now was rumors. And no one wanted to make accusations or retaliate until the truth had been confirmed. The entire region was in a position of delicate instability. Exactly the wrong time to be taking a civilian to Jolo Island.

Riley strode toward the coffee kiosk and admired the very fine butt waiting in line for a moment before he realized he was ogling Diana. Shit.

He rubbed a hand through his hair. That was the last thing he needed. But perversely, the fact that she didn't seem to like him made him want to try harder. He sidled up behind her just in time to hear her moan after she took a sip of her steaming coffee.

The sound went straight to his dick. He shifted his bag in front of his groin and hoped no one noticed his raging hard-on. It was going to be a long fucking trip if her unguarded response to coffee instantly made him hard.

"Good morning," he rumbled in her ear and smiled as the puff of breath caused goosebumps to rise on her neck and her nipples to pucker beneath another form-fitting cotton, long sleeve shirt. In theory the shirt wasn't remotely sexy, but the way the thin waffle weave clung to her high, perfect breasts and shaped to her flat, taut stomach revealed far more than it concealed. And her well-worn khaki cargo pants hung low on her sharp hip bones and cupped her absolutely spectacular ass. Riley's palms itched with the desire to run his hands over her curves.

Diana yelped and bobbled her coffee.

Riley cupped his hand underneath hers like he was bracing his weapon, so she didn't spill the hot liquid. "Easy," he murmured. "You don't want to get burned."

Her pale pink, unpainted lips tightened and Riley tried, really hard, not to notice the flawless bow and think X-rated thoughts.

He couldn't help but want to rile her until she unclenched her teeth and let him have it. Even her arguing made him hard. Riley let his fingers skim the inside of her forearm as he removed his hand from hers, the touch in no way inappropriate but still sensual as hell.

Her only response was a tight, "Thank you."

"Have a seat and I'll see if Shane and Ethan are almost ready to go." Riley glanced at his Luminox Point Man watch, checking the time, and ignoring the inbuilt compass. "The pallets were loaded last night, so once we file our flight plan and gas up, we should be good to go."

"Can't wait," Di said coolly, clearly meaning the exact opposite. She skedaddled to the row of plastic chairs as if she couldn't stand to be near him, and sat primly in the hard seat. Then she pulled out her smart phone and proceeded to ignore him.

Riley took one more second to admire her outdoorsy look, woven hemp bracelets loose on her wrists, cargo pants low on her hips, and the tight Henley. With rectangular navy glasses that accented her gorgeous eyes, she looked like the epitome of every smart chick in high school who looked down her nose at him—at least it felt that way—when he'd barely scraped by with a C and she'd set the curve.

But he'd always managed to sweet talk the smart girls

out of their glasses and their panties with ease, playing into every single bad boy fantasy they dreamed up after they finished studying. So who was really the smart one?

Riley suppressed a grin and tried really hard not to get turned on by her snarky attitude but he didn't succeed. Every time she pursed those lips, he wanted to lick into her mouth and spend the twelve or so hours of the long flight exploring her body. His cock rose as he thought about all the time they had before they arrived on Jolo Island and started the next, more grueling leg of their trip.

Now who was the one with the fantasy?

Which was exactly that. A fantasy. Once he started laying down the ground rules, she'd have even less interest in getting busy with him than she did now. Riley confirmed with Shane that they were only about half an hour from takeoff. Then he sauntered to the bank of seats and eased down next to her. Riley gave her his best smile. The one that got him the biggest piece of pie in the restaurant or the key to an upgraded suite in his hotel.

"We can board in a few minutes," he told her.

She rolled her eyes then redirected her gaze back down at the screen on her phone, dismissing him as if he were a particularly pesky fly. "Fine."

Damn, that smile usually worked.

"Is there a reason that you don't like me?" He had tried to figure out why and failed to come up with any other reason than she was pissed because he hadn't wanted her to go on this trip. He still thought it was a bad idea, but he and Jack had come up with measures to keep her safe.

"I don't dislike you," she disagreed.

"That's not what I asked." Riley tried to temper his reply but he really didn't get it. As far as he knew, he hadn't done anything to her personally, besides try to keep her safe.

He couldn't even process why his blood pressure seemed to elevate around her. He was known for his calm under pressure and his easygoing attitude, but Di Lundberg got on nerves he didn't even know he had. He shrugged off his ire. But with her acerbic attitude and unprovoked animosity, it was going to be a really long trip.

"Have you had your inoculations?" Ha, he might have found a way past having to take her with him. The thought had him relaxing slightly.

"Nice try, hotshot." She smirked. And even that little curl of her sexy mouth turned him on. "Yes, I'm up to date on all my shots."

Birth control immediately popped into his head. He cocked a saucy eyebrow at her. "All of them?"

Di rolled her eyes again. "Really?"

"It's going to be a long trip," he said with another suggestive smile.

No bites at all. Riley knew he was trying too hard but he was so thrown off by the fact that she wasn't falling for his charm that he couldn't help it. He was overthinking this. And why did he care? Women usually fell at his feet. So what was it about her dismissive attitude that made him want to press up into her personal space and make her admit that she was attracted to him?

He knew when a woman wasn't interested. But she was usually still receptive to his particular brand of charm. Not Di. She resisted everything he threw at her. However, her body didn't lie.

Physically, she responded every time he was near enough to kiss her. Her pupils dilated, her nipples peaked, and her cheeks flushed. She tried to disguise her reaction with temper but he recognized the signs.

And he couldn't help but try and provoke her.

Huh. The response was so odd and out of character he hesitated for a moment. What the hell? But if she wasn't interested in him, he might as well make it official. She was going to flip a lid once he was done giving her his conditions for traveling on Jolo Island. "While we're waiting, we need to go over the rules once we hit the Jolo Airport."

"What rules?" she asked suspiciously.

And he got down to business. "Once we are in country, I am the law. If I tell you to duck, you duck. If I tell you to stay in the room, you stay. Whether you like me or not, I know what precautions need to be taken to keep you safe so we can deliver these supplies without any incidents. I can't be hampered by worrying if you're going to ignore my directions."

With every word he uttered, her body had gotten stiffer and stiffer. He had known she wouldn't like what he had to say. But since she insisted on coming with him, she was going to follow his rules. Or she was going to find herself hog-tied and on a plane back to the U.S. without stepping foot out of the Jolo Airport.

"Are you freaking serious?" She carefully set her coffee on the little Formica table between the two banks of chairs and stood. She jammed her fists on her hips and then cocked her head as if she were going to go off on him.

Riley crowded closer to her, using his larger body and slightly taller height to try to physically intimidate. At six one he was the shortest of his brothers and yet still damn tall. But when she stood, they were almost nose to nose. It was disconcerting as he tended to date women much shorter than him and far more petite. And why his mind went straight to women he dated, he didn't know. But she was so close he could feel the heat emanating off her, and practically see the steam coming out her ears.

And the urge to grab her and plant a hot, carnal kiss on those lips was nearly overwhelming. She'd be a damn handful in bed, and her lean, muscled body would fit his like they were two pieces of a puzzle.

"You insisted on coming along," he rebutted before she even got started.

"I need to come, they're my contacts, they won't deal with just anyone."

"Your contacts. My rules." Riley's tone brooked no refusal. "No compromises, and no arguments."

She opened her mouth to object. He tried to ignore the lush, rounded bow of her lips. For such a rigid, high strung, intensely focused woman, she had the most delicately feminine X-rated mouth he'd ever seen.

Riley held his palm up, right in her face, in the classic, 'talk to the hand' gesture. "Not. Negotiable."

For a moment, he wished she'd stick out her tongue and lick right along the center of his palm.

Instead she nodded curtly, and dropped back down into the hard plastic chair without a word.

That went well.

THREE

*D*i had thought she'd have to fend off Riley Stone the entire twelve hour flight to Jolo, but to her relief, and maybe tiniest disappointment, he sat up in the cockpit with the pilot, Shane, and co-pilot, Ethan. Fortunately she'd brought her Kindle along and after she reviewed their projected delivery routes and the timeline to get all the school supplies where they needed to be and calculated the time they would need to get to the most remote village for her secret and most important delivery, she decided to read a romance.

Di refused to defend her reading choices to anyone. Books had saved her. Growing up she'd been the odd girl out in so many ways, but through books she learned to embrace her own individuality and learned about worlds outside her own.

And she *loved* romances, even if she wasn't even close to the romance novel heroines with their perfect bodies, full breasts, and classic beauty. She loved to read about the developing relationship between two people. And maybe she hadn't found her hero yet, but she had faith she would.

She didn't need the perfect man, the gorgeous, wealthy, experienced guy. She wanted the *right* guy. She wanted a man who had similar interests, who felt passionately about making a difference, who would love her for who she was, and nothing else. She wanted to connect with a man on a level so profound that it was intangible and untouchable.

Of course she'd had relationships. Starter relationships to figure out what she liked in a man and what she didn't. She really thought she'd fall for an intellectual type like Geoffrey, her first long-term boyfriend, grad student and environmental activist. But after awhile he'd bored her to tears.

She'd tried accountants, tech guys, even a scientist. She'd even been engaged once. Each relationship had definitely taught her what she didn't want.

And maybe, just maybe, she'd had the hope when she'd met Jack Stone that he would be accompanying her to the island of Jolo at the bottom of the archipelago. He was everything she finally realized that she appreciated in a man: large, alpha, gruff, a little awkward, and the tiniest bit sweet.

You couldn't always see the sweetness but it was there.

Instead she was stuck with Mr. Suave and Superficial. The kind of guy who thought he could charm his way into and out of situations. She knew the type. She'd almost married one. Until she figured out that hot glances and meaningless words didn't mean true love. It meant she had some use to him.

Riley Stone would just as likely use her as discard her, and she could never be sure if there wasn't some ulterior motive in his actions. What you saw, definitely wasn't necessarily what you'd get. Give her a straightforward, honest, emotional cripple vs. a guy who could manipulate any situation to get what he wanted.

Unfortunately, as she read the very steamy sex scene in her current novel, her brain kept substituting Jack's younger, more annoying brother in place of the hero, until finally Di put her Kindle away and tried to sleep. She wasn't interested in Riley Stone. She wasn't. He was a smooth, smarmy playboy who likely had more than one woman in every port.

So why every time she closed her eyes did she see Riley, his sleek body in a tux, top buttons undone, showing just a peep of muscles through the V in his shirt, and an impressive bulge in the front of his exquisitely tailored pants?

Ugh. She squirmed in the surprisingly luxurious passenger seats at the front of the Lockheed C-130 Hercules cargo plane and attempted to clear her mind and get some rest.

Di finally fell asleep. And dreamed. Riley, smiling and sensual, starred in her fantasies as he kissed a path along the side of her neck, his hot wet mouth finding her erogenous zones, the tender curve of her neck where it met her shoulder, the hollow of her throat, and the sensitive dip on the inside of her elbow. She could feel him smiling as he kissed his way over her skin.

He blew a breath in her ear, and her nipples pebbled. Her breasts grew heavy as he trailed his large hands over her body teasing her with firm strokes and sensual squeezes but never touching her where her body craved his touch. Finally, he palmed her breasts and lavished his attention on the sensitive mounds.

Their clothes melted away and they were skin to skin. She reveled in the hot press of his naked body as he wrapped his muscled arms around her and anchored her to him. One hand was on her butt, the other twisted in her hair, her breasts flattened against his pecs, and his thick hairy thigh pressed between hers, rubbing against her sex and rocking her to orgasm.

The throaty moan was what woke her and Di fidgeted in her seat as she realized her subconscious brain had substituted Riley for the hero in her dreams. Di squared her shoulders and shook her head to dispel the lingering images of Riley Stone and her twined together as he blew her mind and sent her soaring into the sexual stratosphere.

And as she felt the vibration of the plane she realized that their descent and the lowering of the wheels was what had truly awakened her.

Thank goodness, no one else had been in the passenger area to hear her.

They landed at the Jolo Airport in a torrential downpour. Di peered out the window but it was impossible to see anything but sheets of rain. She wasn't even sure how Shane had done it. Although *tag-ulan* usually lasted thru November, the heavy rain of the rainy season was supposed to be over. That's why she'd waited until late November to visit and bring the supplies.

Just one more detail about this trip that was not going in any way according to plan.

"Hello, sunshine." Riley stretched his arms over his head and arched his back, the black t-shirt pulled from the waist of his cargo pants and shot tantalizing glimpses of a hard, eight pack. She wouldn't have guessed his muscles were that defined. His shirts were just the slightest bit loose and his pants a little baggy and failed to emphasize his clearly muscular physique beneath those concealing clothes.

"Did you have a good nap?" He smiled lazily and Di couldn't help the embarrassed flush that crept up her face. Hopefully he'd mistake the color for the close air of the stuffy plane.

Riley didn't say a word but his gaze sharpened as he observed his surly passenger.

If he wasn't mistaken, and he wasn't because damn, he knew women—she was aroused. The pink on her sharp cheekbones deepened.

"Sweet dreams?" he asked languidly, and wondered what in the hell she'd been dreaming about.

Di unbuckled from the beat up leather seat and stood abruptly. "I'd like to use the restroom before we deplane." The Jolo Airport bathrooms tended to be small and weren't always the cleanest.

"Good idea." Riley nodded. "I need to coordinate with Shane to get the pallets offloaded to the storage facility. Can you help us out when you're done?"

Part of reason she needed GHR was because she didn't have a huge shipment. Jolo was a smaller island and didn't need the amount of supplies needed to ship on a shipping container. And sending the pallets commercial cargo was too expensive.

At this point, Riley seemed almost businesslike as he spoke to Shane, his fists propped on his narrow hips as they discussed the best way to offload the supplies from the plane to the truck and the storage area. They were going to have to use the airport storage facilities to hold the extra pallets and make several trips in country using Jolo city as their home base.

Di came back out of the lavatory and headed toward the two men. Shane glanced her way with an easygoing smile that revealed crooked white teeth in a round, black face. Instinctively Di smiled back. His biceps strained the short-sleeved flight suite he wore and emphasized the corded muscles in his arms. Was every man at GHR hot?

Di fought the urge to fan herself.

Riley shoved the clipboard with their delivery itinerary and daily schedule in her hands. "We're going to inspect the pallets and mark them. Can you read the schedule as I go?" For once he wasn't smiling, he was frowning.

"How about you read it and I'll help Shane mark them?" She raised an eyebrow, her bitch quotient rising, as once again Mr. Perfect rubbed her the wrong way. Di smiled at Shane.

"Shane needs to get some shuteye so he can load up and return home in the morning." His abrasive attitude took her by surprise. Mr. Suave was showing some cracks in his happy go lucky demeanor.

Di shrugged. "Fine."

"Thank you," Riley replied shortly. Then he visibly reined in his temper, and reverted back to his more laid back persona.

Di read off the list of schools and towns they were going to visit. She had numbered the pallets before they left so that it should be easy to identify which supplies went to which villages and schools.

She faltered briefly, so briefly, hopefully neither Riley or Shane noticed when she rattled off the last school.

"We have an extra set of supplies." Riley frowned as he stared at the last pallet. The special delivery. The reason she had to make this trip. Now.

Di's heart beat harder against her breastbone. "No. We're good." The slight tremble in her body didn't reflect in her voice at all, as she visualized a calm placid lake. She'd perfected her lying voice years ago when she and Lailani would lie to Sister Maricel, insisting that their mothers wanted them to help with the laundry, and instead they would sneak out to the river to play hooky.

Sister Maricel had always gazed at them suspiciously but

she'd never caught them in the lies and since they had actually helped with the wash, their mothers had never ratted them out.

But Riley snapped his head around and pinned his laser gaze on her. He prowled over to her, moving so much like a predator that mesmerized its prey that she was caught in his knowing, accusatory gaze.

Di's mouth dried as she stared into his jade and amber eyes, sinful, rich and critical. "What are the extra supplies for, Diana?" he asked silkily, his tone suffused with a pleasantry that was noticeably absent from his body language.

Every muscle stood out in harsh relief, the illumination from the overhead lights, shone down on his body, his chest seemed bigger, harder, his pectorals strained against the black t-shirt, his biceps stretched the hem of the short sleeves, even his neck seemed thicker, as if every muscle were tensed, ready for aggression.

His face, highlighted by the harsh lights, was set in brutal lines. The charming, smiling playboy had disappeared. In his place was a warrior. And he was not happy with her right now. "What aren't you telling me?"

She held her breath, held her ground, and stared straight into his judgmental cold gaze. Her heart triple-timed in her chest at sense of menace he exuded. "Nothing." But the word escaped in a puff of breath, more sexpot than firm denial.

Di swallowed.

"Either you tell me, or you go back to the States with Shane and Ethan." The sensual lips that had enticed and cajoled and smiled a few weeks ago were tightened by an anger so fierce it nearly pulsed in the still, tense air of the cargo hold.

Di refused to cower in the face of his ire. If she refused to be charmed by his lazy sensuality and blatant male interest, then she certainly wasn't going to be swayed by his fury. "You can't refuse to take me." She'd made sure that was in the contract.

"I can if the client, that would be you," he snarled, "lies to the GHR employee, that would be me, and knowingly puts the client or the company in danger."

"We're not in danger," she scoffed. Although that was likely true, no one could guarantee that island of Jolo was completely safe. Nowhere on earth was totally safe.

"Really?" Riley stalked closer until Di's back was slammed up against the shrink-wrapped pallet so tightly the hard corners of the ten-year-old encyclopedias dug into her lower back.

She straightened her spine but if she moved even an inch, or breathed too deeply, she'd be pressed up against his hard, intense muscles. He was so close the heat from his body wrapped around her senses. He was up in her grill physically, very intimidating, and not the least bit charming. His surface persona was eradicated by rage. Even with all that anger simmering in him she should be recoiling or at least a little nervous, instead her body to responded to his nearness as if he were trying to seduce her. Her core softened, her nipples hardened into painfully tight buds, and tingles cascaded through her like she was a lightning rod and he was a bolt of electricity.

Clearly he wasn't feeling any of that as he narrowed his striking eyes—a warm amber surrounded his pupils and the color bled to a deep fractured jade—and loomed over her menacingly. "You have an in with the Moro National Liberation Front that you'd like to share with us?"

Di blinked. Her mind stuttered at his nearness. Usually

she was taller than the men around her, not close to the same height which she was with Riley. But somehow his anger had morphed him into a larger, more physically intimidating man.

She needed to push away the unwanted attraction and focus on Riley Stone and placating him so that she was still a part of the delivery of the supplies. She had to get the school supplies to Lailani's *sitio*. And she couldn't do that if Riley blocked her from accompanying him on the delivery route. Dammit.

She did have somewhat of an in with the MNLF, at least with Magtanggol, the husband of her friend, but she certainly wasn't about to share with 'angry Riley'. Magtanggol wouldn't hurt her. He supported Lailani's efforts to improve the school in their village.

"Of course not." She put on her best sweet, 'donate to my cause' smile, swallowed her natural impulse to argue, and shifted her gaze so that she wasn't staring directly into his. "But the government and the MNLF have a peace accord in place right now. We'll be safe."

"You've got to be shitting me." He shifted back on his heels, his intense regard pulled her gaze back to his. He stared into her eyes, his gaze compelling and penetrating, before he looked up and to the right over her shoulder.

"What?" Di tried to turn around, ostensibly to see what he was looking at. She succeeded in breaking the connection, nearly visible in its intensity, that seemed to crackle between them.

In that moment, Riley knew she was lying. Her pale eyes were wide and she was trying so hard to keep her expression even that she forgot she usually looked at him with a sneer. She hadn't looked at him this way, ever. The sheer fact that she *wasn't* trying to bluster and argue her way out of his question was the most damning of tells. If she didn't have anything to hide, she'd be ripping him a new one.

"You totally just lied to me." The veneer of his charm slipped exponentially as she opened her mouth to lie again.

Di frowned, her brown sugar brows cranked into a V and her body morphed into supplication. "I need to go with you." It was probably as closed to begging as she got. She still worked that haughty disdain, it was likely ingrained, but he was pretty sure she was so busy trying to get him to agree to let her go that she wasn't thinking about the attitude she projected.

"Look, hotshot. The last school gets two pallets delivered. It's bigger than the other schools." Her body language screamed distress, as if something catastrophic would happen if she was sidelined. For a brief moment, Riley was distracted by the almost pathological need to soothe her. And he had to wonder, again, what was so important that she would put herself in possible danger.

"Okay," he said slowly. Two pallets for one school. Why didn't she just say say so earlier?

Riley still thought something was off. He knew there was nothing more controversial than sharp pencils contained in the various shrink-wrapped pallets. He'd inspected the contents of her shipment himself, just to make sure, because she'd been so insistent that she had to come on this trip. Riley had been suspicious from the get go. But he'd found nothing subversive or potentially worrisome, so what the hell was going on? "Then why are you so—"

"My contacts are suspicious of strangers," she said almost desperately. "They've been tricked by soldiers and governments before."

Inside, Riley jolted but he carefully kept his face impassive. He wasn't just delivering the school supplies. He had another secret mission for Stone Consulting, which was to get as much intel on the actual sentiment in the villages about the newly minted peace accord and whether or not it would succeed. To ferret out if the Philippine government was as accepting of the accord as they appeared. To find out if the MNLF really intended to stick to the terms or if the current agreement was just a ploy to buy time before they launched another offensive against the reigning government.

So in a sense, he was deceiving the population. And if her contacts were already skittish, he might not be able to learn as much as he needed to make the report worthwhile.

Riley analyzed the pros and cons of making the rest of the journey without her. And he came to the uncomfortable conclusion that he needed her to come along.

But he wasn't about to let Diana know that he needed her.

Fine. You can go." He acted as if he were doing her a favor rather than using her to advance his own personal agenda. He used his charm voice and his standard smile to attempt to put her at ease.

But instead of her normal reaction to his attempted charm, she released her breath and smiled. "Thank you."

Which told him he was right. He couldn't trust her.

FOUR

The next morning, Di waited in the De Mazenod Hotel lobby for Riley. She still wasn't sure what had happened yesterday. She'd seen the calculation and the temper simmering in his gaze. He'd been one minute away from shoving her back on that plane.

Even now, she was figuratively holding her breath. Shane and Ethan hadn't left yet. They needed another few hours on the ground before they would be cleared for the return flight.

Shane and Ethan had to pick up a load of airplane parts from an SAE, Stone Aeronautical Engineering, plant in Manila and then they were heading back to the U.S. It was another reason that GHR had been able to pay for Di's freight to Jolo. They could piggy back the delivery of her supplies to Jolo with the export of SAE's goods back to the U.S.

Shane and Ethan had already left for the small airport but it wasn't so far away that Riley didn't have time to get her on the plane back to the U.S. if he so chose.

Riley had gone from combative to speculative to in a

rapid-fire switch. And while she was thrilled that he finally acquiesced, the reasoning behind his agreement was making her nervous. What was he up to? Did she care? He agreed to let her come along. And right now that had to be her main goal.

"Morning." His breath puffed along the back of her neck sending a shower of tingles through her traitorous body. Her mind might protest his particular charm, but her body reacted to Riley Stone like he was her crack.

Di whirled around and her breath backed up in her chest. He smelled of shave cream, soap, and some earthy musk that was likely uber-expensive cologne. Her heart picked up its pace and her body buzzed with a combination of adrenaline and arousal.

Last night in her room she'd convinced herself that he really wasn't as attractive as she'd thought. That her body didn't quiver with longing every time he got up in her personal space, which oddly seemed to happen on a regular basis.

"You ready," she asked brusquely, trying to mask her unwilling hunger for him. It was only lust, she dismissed. Who wouldn't be attracted to such a hot package? Unfortunately, there was nothing behind the gorgeous face and muscled body to warrant more than emotionless passion.

"We've got a schedule to keep." Riley tapped his extremely complicated looking watch. "Truck is ready and loaded. Let's go."

Di let out an easy sigh of relief. He wasn't going to try to send her back home.

∼

They bounced over a rough road. Riley consulted the GPS on his watch regularly. His hands on the wheel of the truck were loose but steady as he navigated the irregular terrain and barely travelable roads to the first school on their delivery schedule.

They'd been on the road for about an hour. The cab of the truck had been mostly silent as they ate a *Pankaplog* breakfast consisting of small bread rolls called pandesal, eggs, and coffee from the *tapsihan* next to their hotel.

"So these contacts of yours...." Riley checked the rear view mirror, then the side mirror, then focused on Di. He needed information. "How do you know them?"

She leaned back against the passenger door, and stared out at the encroaching jungle. "I grew up here."

Succinct. To the point and not really an answer. Huh. Was that on purpose?

"Really?" Riley gripped the wheel tightly as he used brute force to turn the truck to the right. The power steering was either out or hadn't been invented when the ancient truck was built. On the plus side, the engine ran like a dream, so he couldn't really complain. "Parents in the military?"

"Missionaries," she replied shortly.

Riley raised an eyebrow at the slightly hostile tone. "Admirable work." He really couldn't understand why the animosity. He turned up the wattage on his smile, but it went to waste as she hadn't looked at him since they had begun their journey this morning. He was determined to draw her out. "Are they still here?"

"No. They retired to Branson, Missouri. They build houses in the Appalachian mountains every spring."

Still apparently dedicating their time to worthy causes.

Which still didn't quite explain how Diana had made her contacts or why she was here.

"Why school supplies?" Maybe if he could get her talking about her passion, he'd crack the hard shell that isolated her and kept her from engaging with him.

She was starting to get more involved in the conversation. She'd shifted straighter in her seat, her rigid spine relaxed and her hands moved as she spoke about her company. "The kids frequently get caught in the crossfire of the warring factions on the island," Di said grimly. "I can't tell you how many schools have been destroyed by errant bombs or guerrilla fighting in the area."

Riley knew all about the problems with village infrastructure becoming collateral damage in wars. "Yeah, I saw plenty of examples of that when I was in the Navy."

"Well, this is my contribution to helping the villages maintain stability and procuring supplies for their schools." Her cheeks had flushed and her eyes were bright as she talked about what Tools for Schools was doing. "Every delivery we make helps these kids have opportunities, helps show these kids that there are other things out there, other *worlds* out there."

A commendable goal. And one that Riley was behind one hundred percent. Not that she would believe him if he told her that. But he understood better than she'd ever know about empowering kids.

"It sounds like you're doing a lot of good," he said neutrally.

Before he could say more, they rounded the bend and came upon the first school on their delivery schedule.

Di bounded from the truck before he could caution her about sticking with him until he cleared the location. She had been correct that schools were destroyed all the time.

Riley needed to make sure this was a safe area first. "Dammit, Di, wait."

Riley checked his weapon and vaulted out of the truck but it was already too late.

Di and a short woman, slim build, and thick straight black hair, were jumping up and down and hugging each other tight. He strode toward the pair. He took a quick glance around just to make sure no danger lurked in the encroaching jungle.

"Christina Chua, this is Riley." Di introduced them. "He's helping me deliver the supplies this run."

Christina Chua was clearly a mestizo, mixed Chinese, Filipino and likely some other ethnicities thrown in. She had wide high cheekbones, slightly tilted dark eyes, and a sweet smile as she bowed. "Pleased to meet you, Riley."

Riley smiled. "Likewise." He glanced around, noted the cracked cement pad that lead to the small, one room schoolhouse. Weeds sprouted between the cracks and paint peeled on the metal slats of the converted double wide trailer.

He felt very exposed and out in the open.

While Di and Christina caught up, a little boy peered around Christina's sarong dress and stared at Riley with large brown, heavily-lashed eyes. Riley's frown softened. When he was assured that it was safe, he beckoned the boy toward the truck.

The two women were chattering a mile a minute in Tagalog, and so caught up in each other that they were unaware of anything else. Riley holstered his weapon and strode back to the truck. He dragged his duffel from behind the driver's seat and unzipped it quickly.

Besides the SAT phone, first aid kit, extra socks, extra pencils, extra magazines for his pistol, and extra shells for his shotgun in his backpack, he'd brought along some gifts for the kids. He continued to monitor their surroundings as he pulled a deflated soccer ball from the bag and a small portable pump. With efficient movements, he began to inflate the ball.

The little boy grinned, revealing two large gaps where he'd lost his baby teeth. His brown eyes sparkled and his face reflected his happiness. Once the ball was hard enough, Riley tossed the pump back in the bag. He threw the ball in the air and then sent it flying toward the boy with a solid header.

The little guy laughed and chased after the ball. Once he rounded the other side, Riley made a 'bring it' gesture with his left hand, careful to keep his right hand free, and to stay aware of their surroundings.

The kid kicked the ball hard. Riley stopped it with his chest, let it drop to the packed dirt, and then executed a fancy one-two kick, not too hard and grinned as the boy raced after the soccer ball.

He was still grinning when he chanced a look at the two women. They stood close together, arms wrapped around each other's waists, and their mouths hanging open. The local woman radiated sheer approval, but in that moment, Riley could care less. He wanted to know what Di was feeling.

Di was watching him speculatively, no smile in place. But there was a softness around her eyes that he thought might mean she approved. Riley couldn't even figure out why he cared. But he was self-aware enough to acknowledge that he did care what she thought of him. Far more than he should.

Di watched Riley kick the soccer ball back and forth with Christina's son. Her first, cynical thought was that of course he would charm a small child. But when a big grin lit

up his face and his hazel eyes sparkled with sheer enjoyment, she acknowledged that he was engaged purely for the pleasure of both Michael and himself. She forced herself to let go of the instinctive need to belittle his charm. It didn't speak well of her at all. And the emotion that burned through her chest was shame. She certainly shouldn't begrudge Riley for thinking of the kids.

Riley knelt down so that he was eye level with Michael and spoke softly to him. But Di noticed that Riley constantly monitored the area. Even while he was playing with Michael, he kept scanning the school area and the surrounding jungle for threats. She certainly appreciated his diligence.

"Okay, little man." Riley stood quickly, his powerful thighs bunched and flexed beneath the cargo pants. He strode to the back of the delivery truck. With efficient movements he opened up the back gate and hopped into the truck. Riley sliced through the shrink-wrap with an efficient and deadly looking knife. Then he began to lift the school's supplies off the back of the truck. "Have fun with the ball. I'll play later."

She thought about letting him know that several villagers would be along in about fifteen minutes to unload the truck but Di was struck by his rippling arm muscles as he hefted a particularly heavy box of encyclopedias onto his shoulder. Her throat went dry and she swallowed down the urge to moan at the subtle display of his power.

He wasn't even trying right now and she was practically melting into a puddle of desire at his feet. She tried to dredge up some scorn, he was posturing, all part of his macho charm machine. But no one was watching except Michael and Di. Christina had gone into the trailer, the single building of this local 'school', to make sure there was room to store the boxes before they were unpacked.

Di decided to fill him in on what was happening, and strode over to Riley. "We have some locals coming to unload the truck if you'd rather wait."

"I don't mind getting started." Riley shifted the box on his shoulder. "I'd rather get everything into the school before night falls."

Di grabbed a smaller box and kept pace with him as they hoofed to the door of the school. "How did you know to bring the soccer ball?"

Riley shifted his attention to her face before he tilted his head and answered, "Kids need play too. Especially those kids who struggle with the books. They need a place to succeed."

Wow. She certainly wouldn't have thought he'd be that insightful. "Who would have thought Riley Stone was so sensitive?" The mocking words came out of her mouth before she could sensor them.

"Yeah, well, everyone is full of surprises," Riley said shortly. "Who would have thought that someone who has the compassion to deliver school supplies to underserved kids could be such a bitch?" He said the words with a smile on his face, his expression didn't falter, and if she had been watching without sound, she would have had no idea about the sting in his words. That was what he was good at, she reminded herself, putting on an act. But that still didn't excuse her behavior.

Remorse filled her. She *was* being a bitch. What was wrong with her? It wasn't his fault that his charming exterior pushed all of her bitch buttons. It was her problem not his. "Riley." Di placed her hand on his bicep to stop him. "I'm sorry."

His arm flexed beneath her palm, hot and hard. "Fine."

"No really." God, she felt terrible. "I really am sorry. That was completely uncalled for."

"Forget about it." But he'd turned his head away so that she couldn't see his face and she was pretty sure that she'd hurt his feelings.

"Let's get these supplies unloaded so we can get back on the road," Riley said coolly. He could have been speaking to a stranger.

"Ummm, can we stay for dinner?" Di trotted alongside him as he carried the box into the classroom.

"Traveling on the roads at night isn't advisable." Riley swung the box down to the floor in the corner where Christina had cleared an area for the supplies to be stored until she could get them set up in the 'classroom'.

The old metal trailer was outfitted with handmade bookshelves, desks that hailed from the early 70s, and an ancient blackboard. Christina had spruced up the walls with posters of the alphabet, a world map that was about ten years out of date, and some *Dora the Explorer* posters. The floor was threadbare carpet repaired with duct tape and the walls were scuffed and marked up. But they had books of all persuasions and Riley knew that besides the encyclopedias, and other reading books, this shipment contained paper and pencils, even some colored pencils.

"It's not much," Di said desperately.

"This is better than some," Riley spoke as if from experience. "And with your supplies, they are even better stocked than other schools I've seen."

"Yes." She watched him cautiously.

Her heart burned and she wanted to call back her earlier caustic words and get that easygoing grin back on his face. But she feared that she'd ruined his good mood permanently.

A commotion from outside clattered into her consciousness. Riley reacted in an instant and removed his weapon from the holster with one fluid movement. He held up his palm, then pressed his arm back against her torso. "Stay here, and take cover behind the desk."

That seemed a little extreme. "It's probably just the men coming to help unload the supplies."

"Rules, Di." He shot her a censorious look. "Probably. But you pay me to protect you from threats."

Actually, she didn't. Another pang of remorse shot through her. GHR was donating so much of their own resources to this mission that she wasn't paying him a dime.

Riley stood to the left of the large picture window, moved the curtain slightly with the barrel of the gun to peer outside the small trailer. His hands were capable and strong on the grip and his body was taut with anticipation.

"Looks like it's the delivery boys." After a few seconds, he relaxed and let the curtain drop. "How sure are you about your friends?"

"They aren't my friends," Di protested. "But Christina is my friend and she vouches for them."

"And how sure are you of Christina, because for guys who are just here to unload school supplies, they are very heavily armed." Riley pivoted on his heel. "I go out first."

Di noted that he kept his hands firmly on his weapon and the expression in his eyes was far from welcoming. In that moment, he looked like the warrior he was. Oh, he hid it well under exquisitely-tailored suits and fine Egyptian cotton shirts, but now, stripped bare of the outer trappings of wealth, Riley Stone looked like the muscle she'd hired from GHR.

Di was confident that if Christina trusted the men here to help then they could too. But she also knew that people could turn, loyalties could be broken. Many of the people on this island had little, so it wasn't unheard of for neighbor to sell out neighbor. But she knew that Riley would protect her.

"Okay." Di opened the door. Riley moved so he was still partially protected by the door frame, although rounds from the weapons these guys were carrying would tear through the wood and flimsy metal walls of this trailer.

Riley called out. "Christina, we're coming out. Please make sure none of your friends are trigger happy."

Christina laughed, the sound like water over a brook, sweet and melodious. "You need not worry."

"It's ingrained, honey."

She spoke in Tagalog so quickly that Riley could only pick up every few words. "Did you get that?" he asked Di softly.

"Yes," she replied. "We're fine."

"You sure?"

She nodded. "Look. They're getting the boxes out of the truck."

"Okay." Riley stepped cautiously out of the school and headed for the truck. Christina met him at the back gate and introduced the four men who'd come to help unload the school supplies.

They all shook hands and then began the physical task of emptying the truck. There were four men of varying descents, the one thing they all had in common was the very new, very deadly weapons strapped to their waists. "You have many problems lately?" he asked, aware of the fact that he needed to gather as much information as possible about the conditions and the temperament of the people on the island.

One man who clearly had more Spanish heritage than the rest shrugged. "Things are peaceful. Right now." He spat a thick globule of chew onto the hard-packed dirt.

Another, who was clearly mestizo, a mix of Chinese, Negrita, and White nodded. "But who knows how long it will last," he said in heavily-accented English.

The first shook his head vigorously. "We hope for peace. But we are prepared for more war."

So the feeling, at least in this little *sitio*, was optimistic cynicism.

"The treaty is going well?"

The second glanced left, then right. "Most want peace. Everyone is tired of fighting."

"But?"

"But there are some who don't like the deal, who still believe the government is taking advantage. There are always rumblings."

Not a surprise. This island had been prone to violence and aggression for decades. Riley leaned closer. "We are supposed to deliver in some of the more remote *sitios*. Will we have any problems?"

He'd checked with all of his contacts before coming to Jolo. But situations like the current treaty were fluid and changed constantly. He had no intention of taking Di someplace that would get them both killed. It would be bad for business. And life.

"You will not be harmed," the last one said vehemently.

But after talking with the men, an uneasiness haunted Riley.

Christina lived in a very small house at the back of the property where the school resided. Against Riley's better

judgment, they stayed for dinner. A simple meal of salted fried fish, rice, and yams.

He observed Di interact with her friend. They had clearly known each other for a long time. "How do you know each other?"

"We went to school together." Christina said softly, "Now, I am a teacher and she is our angel."

Di flushed. Unusual for her. But she was softer, less edgy with her friend. Less judgmental, less acerbic.

Riley glanced at his watch. It was getting late. "We should really get back to Jolo city."

"Oh, you must stay for dessert. It is Di's favorite." Christina smiled shyly.

Di laughed. "You made *leche flan*?"

"Of course."

After Diana's tearful goodbye with Christina, they rode back to Jolo in silence. Riley was thinking about the men's revelations about the political climate on the island. There was something about the men's demeanors that struck a warning in his gut. He'd learned over the years to trust his intuition. He might not be the sharpest at certain things, so he'd learned to rely on his abilities. They needed to proceed very carefully. "Did Christina mention anything about the current political climate or feelings on island?"

"We didn't discuss politics."

"So you didn't ask at all about what the general mood was surrounding the current peace accord?"

"Why?" she asked suspiciously.

"It directly affects the inhabitants of the island." Riley started to get a little steamed. She couldn't be that naive, could she? "If the treaty goes south, everyone here will be thrust back into what amounts to civil war."

"That has nothing to do with my friends."

"Don't put your head in the sand, sweetheart." Riley tapped his fingers on the steering wheel as he contemplated various scenarios. "The success or failure of the treaty affects every single inhabitant of this island."

And if the accord failed in the next few days, it would adversely affect them.

He waited a few beats, then decided his need for information trumped his need to have peace with Di. He would be wise to gather any other intel he could.

"At our next stop, I'd like you to find out what you can."

"What?" Di shifted in her seat so that she was facing him, her back up against the passenger door, and her knee almost touching his hip.

"Are you...." She placed a hand over her heart. "Please tell me you aren't spying on my friends."

He chanced another look at her. Her face was white, and her hands were gripped in a prayer position. He wasn't spying on her friends, per se. But he was definitely collecting information. "Look, my job is to make sure that you're safe while we deliver these supplies. Your friends, like it or not, know more about the current political flow than my contacts. My goal is to get through this job safely without any unforeseen problems." Which was true, insofar as it went. Just because he had another agenda was none of her business.

He knew he should be laying on the charm, trying to cajole the information out of her, trying to sweet talk her suspicions away. But he couldn't make himself do it. He wouldn't lie to her but he also wasn't going to share the truth with her. She already had a shitty opinion of him. No need to make it worse.

Clearly he failed since the rest of the ride was spent in silence.

FIVE

The next three days passed in a strained atmosphere. Riley had given up trying to charm her. She seemed immune to his particular brand of allure, which did not mean she wasn't attracted to him. She was. For which he was happy. He'd hate to be the only one stuck in this sexual limbo. Because every hour spent in the close confines of the truck cab reinforced his unwilling lust for Diana Lundberg.

It was fascinating, really, how he could be so hot for someone who didn't have an inkling of appreciation for him. If he wasn't so confident in his prior relationships, he'd think he was developing a masochistic side.

He'd been in a state of semi-arousal for the past three days and nothing seemed to quell it. Not her acerbic response to anything he did. Not the very clear indication that absolutely nothing would ever happen between them. Not his own stern, silent conversations in his head. He could have any woman he wanted, except apparently Di Lundberg.

So he tried to ignore the attraction that simmered

43

between them and focus on his job. He continued to gather information for his Stone Consulting report, and was more and more amazed at her generosity of spirit—with everyone but him.

They'd visited five more *sitios*, deep in the rural areas of Jolo Island, and with each day his concern grew. There had been no overt signs of hostility against them but he felt as if the jungle and hills had eyes and they were multiplying with each trip to deliver the school supplies. He had kept to the roads along the coast when possible to stay as far away from the terrorist factions that operated in the bowels of the island.

He continued to gather intelligence about the situation on Jolo which was definitely less stable than he'd originally thought. More than once he'd suggested that Di stay at their hotel while he made the deliveries but she'd nixed that idea in seconds. And he hated to admit it but she'd been right. The locals here knew her. She smoothed the way just being her. Which was another surprise. She was so contentious with him, but she was all sweetness and happiness with her Filipino friends.

Di hadn't complained about the conditions, which had grown increasingly worse. She took everything in stride except for him. He was able to charm her friends. And the kids. They'd loved the soccer balls. Just the thought had him smiling.

Riley strode back to the truck and hopped in the back. They had one more pallet of supplies to unload and then they were done. But as he opened his knife and got ready to rip into the wrap holding the supplies on the pallet, the feeling of disquiet grew. The reason his intuition had been going crazy, whatever that might be, was ramped to about a thousand degrees.

Di swung into the back of the truck.

"Let's get this last pallet unloaded and get out of here," Riley said.

Her pale blue eyes avoided his gaze. "Slight change of plans."

"What?"

"We have one more delivery to make. But it's not here."

Riley's temper simmered. This was what had been nagging him. Ever since that confrontation on the plane after they'd landed. He'd been thinking about her evasive gaze when she'd told him that this school was getting two pallets of supplies. He should have pushed harder.

The sense of doom that had hovered like a raincloud burst open and showered him with anger. "Where?"

Di smiled at him. Strike number one. She never smiled at him. Ever.

She smiled vacantly over his shoulder when it was needed but she hadn't made true eye contact since their first school delivery and his impromptu soccer play with Michael Chua.

Which meant something was up. "What?"

She pressed her fingers along her thighs, smoothing the material of her tan cargo pants until no wrinkles marred the surface. "I have the coordinates of the last delivery."

Riley's suspicions raised again. "What are they?"

She gave him the long and lat. After Riley mentally calculated where she wanted to go, his temper exploded. "No fucking way."

"We have to make this delivery."

"You're talking about going into the heart of the Moro National Liberation Territory," he snarled. "Have you been listening to the rumors your friends have been sharing with us?"

"I know that it will be a...delicate situation."

"Are you out of your mind?"

"There's a school there that really needs supplies." She pressed her palms together as if in prayer and she begged. "Seriously. I've watched you with the kids the last few days. You really care."

The surprise in her voice pissed him off beyond reason. "So now you're going to use that against me?"

"These kids have nothing."

"You're talking about driving through the most militant of the Moro National Liberation Front territory. Even if they are committed to peace, they are just as likely to take us hostage as let us through," Riley argued.

"I know," Di countered. "But my best friend is the teacher for the school."

Riley slammed his fist on top of the last pallet. "No fucking way."

"Please Riley," Di begged. Then she gave him the smile that she gave to everyone else. A smile she had never blessed on him.

"Really?"

"What?"

"You actually think you can charm me?" Riley curled his fingers into fists and fought the very strong urge to punch the pallet again. "The very move you scoff at me for regularly and now you're trying it on me?"

"I don't—"

"Yes, you do." Riley jumped down from the back of the truck and stalked to the cab. "What the hell, Di?"

"These kids have nothing."

"I get that but, Jesus." Riley rubbed his hand over his face.

"Which is exactly why this is the most important delivery we have to make."

"You realize that we need more security."

She shook her head. "That's the last thing we need. More security would be perceived as a threat. Taking a single truck with just you and me was the only way we could get into this area to deliver the supplies."

Riley swore. She was probably right. But he'd still like a regiment of soldiers and maybe an RPG. What the fuck?

"Are you suicidal?" he asked pleasantly.

She shook her head. "I have allies in the area. They won't let anything happen to us."

That triggered his memory. When he'd asked her if she had friends in MNLF. This, *this* was that look that she'd given him. How the hell had he let her overrule his natural instincts? Dammit.

"Lailani's husband will escort us." Di said, "We'll have protection. You don't need to worry."

Hell yes, he needed to worry.

"These kids, my friend's daughter, Divina, specifically needs the supplies we've got."

"What is so special about these supplies?" But her answer didn't matter. There was *nothing* that she could say that would get him to acquiesce and go into this particular region.

"Divina is dyslexic." Di said, "I don't know if you know what that—"

"I know what dyslexia is," Riley said shortly. The acid from his stomach roiled and burned as he acknowledged she'd won. With five short words, she'd overturned his objections.

"We have special materials to help her learn to read." Di

continued not realizing he'd already given in. "And educational books on tape."

As if she'd reached inside his mind, she'd found the one weakness he'd buried. He'd been there. Been that kid who'd been made fun of because as hard as he tried, he couldn't make sense of words. With an absentee father, and no mother figure until Shelley came to live with them when he'd been twelve, he'd spent his elementary and middle school years in hell.

He knew he was as smart as other kids. He could take apart a car's guts and put it back together by the time he'd been ten, he could speak Spanish and French by the time he was eleven, he could memorize travel routes and chemistry symbols and do mathematical equations in his head. And without help he'd learned to use his charm to ease out of reading and writing whenever he could. But he'd always sucked at reading.

Once Shelley came to live with them, she'd gotten him some tutoring, but at that point not a lot stuck. He was never going to be a big reader or even proficient at reading. He needed to hear the words to make connections. Dammit. Fuck.

Riley's mind raced. He wouldn't stop the delivery to her friend's school, however he refused to take Di that far in country. But maybe he could find a way to get those supplies to her friend's daughter.

"Compromise. We will meet them and make a transfer. But I will not take you into that zone."

Shit. There were so many ways this could still go wrong. But how could he deny that kid a chance to be successful, a chance to learn?

In the cab of the truck, Di was quiet.

"What's wrong now?"

"I thought you'd take a lot more convincing."

"Well, you thought wrong." Riley was running through scenarios in his head, thinking about potential drop off points, safe routes, and how to transfer the supplies when the heat of her hand on his arm stopped him dead.

Di couldn't believe that Riley had given in so quickly. She'd been sure that they were in for a rip-roaring fight. That's why she'd waited so long to tell him about where the supplies needed to go.

"Thank you," she whispered, gratitude and a tight throat made her voice husky. And then she impulsively leaned over to kiss his cheek. His skin was rough with stubble and abraded her lips as she brushed a quick kiss over his cheek.

He whipped his head toward her. "What was that for?"

The cab of the truck shrank as the intimacy of their positions solidified in an instant. The puff of his breath was sweet with the coconut milk he'd had for lunch. His forearm was supple and warm beneath her palm. A sizzle of electricity burned through her as she realized she was touching him. The air was thick with anticipation and the scent of warm male and musk.

And suddenly the attraction she'd suppressed for the last few days blossomed in her core and spread heat throughout her body. She was frozen in place. Her breasts mere inches from the muscled strength of his bicep as his hands flexed on the steering wheel as if he were anchoring himself to stop from reaching for her.

His eyes were so close she could see the striations of amber in the green and the layer of desire in his hooded gaze.

All the air sucked from the truck, and Di inhaled a quick breath.

Her blood chugged through her veins, slow and

somnolent. As the heat in the truck's cab rose, they both held still, caught in the force field of the attraction that had simmered between them since they met. Di may have tried to shove it down, away, but the truth was she'd spent most of her time with Riley trying to ignore his appeal.

She was leaning almost on his arm, and he didn't move. If she were less confident she might take his stillness as a rejection. But she could literally feel his effort to resist their pull. If the expression in his eyes was any indication, it was taking all he had to hold himself immobile.

His gaze dropped to her mouth. Her lips still tingled from the light brush against his skin and the soft stubble on his face. Her lips and mouth were so dry in spite of the lush tropical air, and she swallowed hard to keep from licking them. But she lost the battle and her tongue came out to wet them.

Riley groaned, and he lifted his hand from the wheel, slowly, carefully, giving her plenty of time to back away. But Di couldn't move. She'd been imagining this moment since she'd caught sight of him in Jack Stone's office over two and a half weeks ago. His large rough palm cupped her cheek, his long fingers threaded through her short curls and a shiver worked its way over her spine.

His callused thumb brushed down her cheekbone and lingered at the corner of her mouth, his gaze firmly glued on her lips.

He gently eased her closer, until their lips were separated by less than a single sheet of paper. They held there suspended, as she waited, he waited, the only sound in the still quiet cab was the erotic sough of their breaths mingling together.

Finally, he pressed his lips to hers, lightly, reverently, tempering the lust that lingered between them. He captured her top lip in his mouth and sucked gently, then he pressed open-mouthed kisses along the outline of her lips, as if he wanted to taste each section, touching searching for the subtle differences between the corners, and the bow, and her fuller bottom lip.

He was barely touching her, only one hand at the nape of her neck, the other still firmly gripped the steering wheel, and still, she was about to go up in flames.

Oh my God.

Riley's fingers slid through the silky curls along the curve of Di's head, as he lost himself in the sensual pleasure of tasting her, testing her, searching out the secret caverns of her mouth, the nip of her teeth as she playfully teased him. The earthy scents of coconut, ylang-ylang blossoms, and some unidentifiable sweet aroma that was uniquely Diana. Her perfume wreathed the cab of the truck and wrapped around his senses. With every inhale, her scent surrounded him, intoxicated him, as he lost himself in the sensual eroticism of her kiss.

Only their mouths were touching. Her lips firm and questing against his. Engaging. Participating.

Definitely not pushing him away.

When he'd pictured kissing her, he'd confess, he'd imagined a frantic, wild, out-of-control passion that finally bubbled over and overwhelmed them both. The tension had been rising between them for days. Riley was pretty sure she didn't even like him but he knew women and her body had responded to his every time they were near each other. He wasn't sure his self-respect wasn't going to take a hard hit because with his track record, he could have anyone he wanted, so why was he so drawn to this woman?

She held a deep disdain for him, no matter what he did, and he had stopped trying to change her mind days ago. For some reason, her complete dismissal of his appeal rankled in ways that he couldn't even figure out. Why did he care if she didn't find him charming?

She might not like him, but she was in lust with him.

So when he'd thought about them together, frequently, he'd assumed their passion would overpower their reservations and they'd couple frantically in the dark and then both wish they hadn't almost immediately after.

But when she'd looked at him with those big, compassionate blue eyes, and her smile lit her face, he'd been overcome with the need to caress her, finesse her reaction, to take care, and show her how much he wanted her.

She held her fists tight against her collarbone as if she were afraid to touch him. In a moment, they needed to stop. They were exposed and unprotected, alone in the clearing in front of the empty school. Anyone could come up on them while they were engaged. And Riley refused to put Di in danger.

He eased back from their embrace, and brushed his thumb over her plumped lips. "We need more privacy than this allows," he said gruffly.

Di stiffened and blinked, as if coming back to herself, then she flushed and pulled away hastily.

Riley opened his mouth to say something, although what he'd pull from his scrambled brain was a mystery, but she held up her palm. "I have the SAT phone. I can call Lailani and tell her about the change of plans."

He pulled out an old-fashioned map of the terrain then consulted the GPS on his watch to confirm the coordinates.

"Okay." He triangulated their position, along with the location of the village where her friend's school was located, and the hotel back in Jolo city. "We rented this truck. If they

take the truck and give us a vehicle to take back to the city, we don't even need to unload the supplies. It can be a quick, even exchange."

Riley pinpointed three locations that would work. "You got them?"

"Yes." Di gripped the Satellite phone with tight fingers and made the call.

He listened as Di spoke with her friend. They agreed to the change in locations fairly quickly and chose the location Riley liked best of the three he'd identified. Maybe it would all work out.

There was only one sketchy area on the way to the meeting place that Riley would be happy to get behind them. After that one section, they should be relatively safe.

Di smiled tremulously as she spoke to Lailani. Once she hung up she said, "They are so thankful."

"Yeah, well, she can thank us after we make the transfer and everything goes okay." Riley tried to keep his tone neutral.

Di fell silent. Riley started up the truck. A light rain began to fall. Great. If this kept up the roads would disintegrate and slow their progress.

"So how does her husband feel about girls getting schooling?"

"Most of the population are fine with girls going to school. The people are slowly coming around to the idea of the girls getting an education." She hesitated. "But it's even harder with kids who suffer from any kind of learning issue."

"Yeah." Riley could imagine. It wasn't always easy in the States, but in a rural area of Jolo Island like her friend's *sitio*, he could see how their educational progress could be measured in small increments.

"You want to talk about it?" she asked tentatively.

The gears ground in a squeal as he shifted into third, trying to push the lumbering truck through the worsening rain. "What?"

"Clearly you have first hand experience with dyslexia."

Riley misdirected. "Hey, I'm a sensitive guy." He gave her his best smile meant to distract and let his gaze roam over her body, trying to shift her focus to sexual. "I watch Oprah."

"Stop that."

He raised a surprised brow. "Stop what?"

"Don't use that fake charm on me."

"I have no idea what you're talking about," he refuted. His charm wasn't fake. But he didn't know her well enough to talk about his learning problems from when he was a kid.

"Right." She huffed and crossed her arms over her chest. The move plumped up her small swells until the bit of cleavage created an intriguing shadow in the V of her t-shirt. "Would it kill you to have a meaningful conversation?"

"I can be meaningful." Riley turned up the wattage on his smile and let suggestion bleed through.

"Forget it." She rested her forehead on the passenger window and turned away, her gaze focused outside the truck, but he knew that wouldn't last long, since there was little to see in the falling rain.

The silence in the truck was deafening. Rain drummed down on the metal roof and the windshield wiper blades punctuated the silence with an admonishing thwap-thwap. As if they knew she was mad at him and wanted to add to his chastisement.

Riley shifted in his seat, trying to avoid the uncomfortable topic. He stretched his left leg, shrugged his shoulders beneath his holster, and glanced at her again.

But she was still staring out the window in disappointed silence.

And finally, he caved unable to bear her displeasure.

"My mother died when I was about two." He never talked about this stuff. Avoided like it was an IED clearly labeled in the middle of the road.

She made a soft noise of sympathy but thankfully kept silent.

"My dad was pretty much...not involved." Riley grimaced. "Jesus, I hate sharing this shit. do we really need to do this?"

"Not at all," Di replied coolly.

Which was girl code for 'if I'm not important enough to discuss this with you then I guess I'm not important at all.'"

And he was insane. Because even sharing wasn't going to get her to like him. But whatever. "I had trouble reading from the get-go. And since I had no mother, the school would tell our nanny, who was banging my father hoping to be Mrs. Stone number two. Honestly, I have no idea if she bothered to share with him or not." With his father, who knew? Maybe the old bastard had known about his learning issues and just didn't care.

"Bitch," Di muttered under her breath. "I'd like five minutes in a room with her."

"She got what she deserved. Which was not Mrs. Stone number two." Riley smiled fondly as he remembered Connor's mother dropping him off on the doorstep. "Dad had knocked up my brother's mom and when Con was about two years old, she decided she'd had enough of motherhood. After Con came to live with us, the nanny figured out she was never going to be Mrs. Stone number two, and decided she didn't sign on for three wild boys."

Di made another sound of disgust, but she had

straightened away from the truck door and turned so she faced him.

"Anyway. Fast forward to when I'm twelve, three more nannies, none of whom became Mrs. Stone number two, but who didn't do much in the way of actually taking care of us either. And I had never been tested, or even gotten extra help, because in order to take those steps, you have to have parental approval."

A genuine smile curved his mouth. "Until Shelley."

"Who is Shelley?"

"My sister's mother. They came to live with us when Jess was eight." Riley recalled the day fondly. "Shelley is still there."

"Mrs. Stone number two?"

"Nope. She refused to marry the old goat. But she insisted on staying to take care of all four of us."

"And she got you help."

It had mostly been too late by the time Shelley marched into the school and demanded they test Riley and get him additional aid. He could read but it was still difficult. Luckily he had the street smarts to get by.

"Yeah."

"So you can relate to Divina."

"Yeah."

"And that's why you brought the soccer balls?" Di's voice had softened, which wouldn't do at all.

Riley might suck at reading. But he was hell on wheels at reading people. And the sweet, soft voice and the relaxing of her body was the picture of surrender.

"And this is where I usually get laid." Riley shot her his best confident, smug smile. "But I'm thinking this is a bad time."

She turned away from him in disgust. Just like he'd

wanted. Riley Stone did not take pity fucks. Not even from women he wanted more than he wanted his next breath.

"Really? You had to ruin this moment with that?"

"What?" He laughed as if he had no cares in the world. "Can't blame a guy for trying."

"So how many girls you really share that story with, hotshot?"

"Enough." *None.* Only Jack had any idea exactly how much trouble Riley had with reading. "But I never kiss and tell, sweetheart."

Di snorted again and turned away from him to stare out the window.

Thankfully, there was no more time to debate his moves. They'd arrived at the exchange destination. Riley shifted the truck into park, and glanced around.

The rain had slowed to a light shower. There was a couple in a car parked at the edge of a long cement pad in front of a small one room municipal building. The little structure was painted a cheery turquoise with white trim and the name of the town painted in black stenciled letters with a four inch band of mosaic tiles trimmed around the front door frame. The sedan in the parking lot had seen better days.

But in the more relaxed culture here, they could switch vehicles with the couple. Then once Di's friends had delivered the school supplies to the school they could drive the truck back to Jolo and exchange it for their car.

The truck rental place would be fine with the car as collateral until their truck was returned. This was a win-win for both parties.

Once again, Di jumped out of the truck without a care for her safety or the danger that could lurk in the jungle. While she might be correct that most on this island would welcome the free school supplies, there were sure to be people who wanted nothing to do with Westerners bestowing charity on their village.

"Di. Dammit. Wait." Riley chambered a round in his weapon, and assessed the cement pad and their surroundings in one quick security sweep. He vaulted to the ground and kept his weapon ready, while he searched for threats.

Di, even after all the discussions they'd had over the last four days, was oblivious as she hugged her friend, Lailani, tightly. Fortunately the husband was equally security-minded. Riley nodded.

"You checked out the area?" he asked in rough Tagalog after they exchanged names and brief nods.

Magtanggol nodded again. "We should hurry."

"That's what I was afraid of," Riley said grimly. "Trade and go."

Di started, "Oh, but—"

Magtanggol shook his head fiercely.

Riley handed him the keys to the truck.

The man gripped his hand tightly and shook. "Thank you for coming." Then he passed over the keys to the ancient sedan to Riley.

"Riley." Di pleaded. Rain ran in rivulets down her face. Riley wasn't sure but he thought she might be crying and he thanked Christ he couldn't tell.

Riley's danger meter was going crazy. They needed to get out of here. Now. "Your friends need to get in the truck. Now. And we need to get out of here."

But before she could carry out his orders, from behind him Riley heard the clicks of multiple weapons being cocked.

"Hands up, lace your fingers together and put your

hands on the back of your head. Do it slowly." The shock of it was the command came from Di's 'friend', Magtanggol. And Riley had no bargaining chip because he'd already handed over the keys. There was nothing to stop them from killing Riley and Di and taking it all. Riley had to hope that wasn't their plan.

"Do it, Di." Riley swore softly but did as he was told. They were outnumbered and very outgunned.

"We're going to sit and have a little chat."

"Magtanggol? Lailani?" Riley couldn't see her but he could hear the confusion, the upset in Di's voice.

Another five soldiers melted out of the woods their weapons trained on Riley and Di. They were surrounded. *Fuck.*

Magtanggol gestured with his weapon, a freaking .357, and as a group they moved toward the little municipal house. Lailani opened the door and gestured for Riley and Di to go inside which Riley took as a good sign. If they were going to kill them they likely would have shot them outside and just dragged their bodies into the jungle.

He still wasn't quite sure how, or if, they were going to get out of this but he'd die trying to save Diana. "Just follow their orders, " Riley commanded softly.

The inside of the little one room structure was clearly a meeting room. There was a long wood plank table with a rough uneven surface and ten crudely-carved wood chairs. Magtanggol shoved the chairs out from the table. "Have a seat. Place your palms flat on the tabletop where we can see them at all times."

"Why don't you just let Diana drive on out of here?" Riley smiled his most charming, non-threatening smile. "For old times' sake."

But no one answered.

The tension in the room slowly tightened as everyone took a seat. Riley absolutely hated the fact that there were six weapons trained on Di.

Lailani had tilted her head and was studying him with a curious expression. She finally said, "We have no quarrel with you."

"Funny. It doesn't look that way from the amount of firepower in the room." Sweat bloomed on his forehead.

"We would be naive and stupid if we didn't treat you as a threat, with your experience and the business you are in."

Riley was more confused than ever but he smiled as if he didn't have a care in the world. "Delivering school supplies?"

"Come Mr. Stone. Ingenuousness does not suit you," Lailani mocked.

"This is a waste of time," Magtanggol said abruptly. "Let's just say we are aware of your other...more covert business."

Riley continued to smile vacuously but inside he was swearing like the sailor he used to be. *Fuck, fuck, fuck.*

"What are you talking about?" Di asked.

Fuckity fuck fuck. For a moment he'd even forgotten about Di.

"We assume that Mr. Stone is also working for Stone Consulting while he delivers your school supplies."

Riley kept silent. But Di, dammit, did not. "Stone Consulting?"

"How do you think Global Humanitarian Relief funds all their good deeds?" Magtanggol continued, putting a nail in his coffin with every word. "It is our guess is that the other arm of the company, Stone Consulting, actually paid for our school supplies to be delivered."

"If you believe that is the case, then why are you holding us at gunpoint?" Riley asked pleasantly.

"One cannot be too careful when dealing with the Stone brothers," Lailani said grimly.

She was right about that.

"Let Di go." Riley wanted those guns off Di now.

"We're going to let both of you go." Lailani steepled her hands together.

Riley wanted to relax but words weren't actions and no one had lowered their weapons. "So what is it that you want?"

"When you communicate with your client. I want you to tell them that MNLF is firmly committed to the peace accord," Magtanggol demanded softly.

"What?" Di queried. "I already know that."

"Now would be a good time to keep quiet, sweetheart."

"Di, my name is Di."

"His other client," Magtanggol said firmly.

Riley calculated the odds that this was some sort of strange trap, but for the life of him, he couldn't see what angle they could be working. If he understood correctly, all they wanted was for him to relay information to the U.S. government. If he went on that supposition, the obvious conclusion was that they were not going to harm either him or Di. They needed them. He nodded slowly giving up the pretense of ignorance. "Okay."

And for once Di was silent.

"We are tired of fighting." Magtanggol shrugged and placed his weapon on the table. Slowly everyone else did the same. "We want our children to grow up in peace. To be able to learn and thrive."

"Why this method of delivering the message?"

"Because while we may want peace and the Philippine government may want peace, there are factions in the military who do not," Magtanggol revealed. "That's what we need your government to know."

Riley shot a furtive glance at Di. Her eyes were wide...and angry. Riley had a feeling all that anger was going to be directed at him and soon.

He'd already gathered intel on the rebels' weaponry, vehicles, and the general state of mind on the island. Their information confirmed what he'd been able to glean from his conversations of the last few days. Most of the rebels really did want peace. "Anything else?"

"Yes. You really are in danger." Magtanggol frowned. "That same faction, the military, has been following your movements around Jolo. Our intelligence says they are going to try to capture you, kill you and blame the rebels, us."

"Well that certainly doesn't appeal to me," Riley said calmly.

"We laid a false trail for them. And I know you have been keeping the truck's owner apprised of your routes each day."

Riley nodded. Thinking it was a good thing he hadn't known about this final delivery, and that he hadn't given the information to the truck's owner, or they'd have been screwed.

Magtanggol pulled out a paper map and spread it over the table. He traced an alternate route back to Jolo with his fingers. "This is the way you need to return."

"Won't that take us straight through the military stronghold?" Riley studied the map.

"It will, but you also have the capability to travel through the jungle, if necessary." Magtanggol meant if they were discovered and pursued by the soldiers. "Plus they will be looking for you in an alternate section of the jungle."

"We will also draw the soldiers away from your route

back to Jolo." Magtanggol smiled. "But we cannot engage them. It would violate the terms of the peace accord. We cannot. You understand this?"

"I do." Riley's temper was starting to simmer. "You planned all of this?"

Lailani and Magtanggol nodded.

Riley shoved his chair away from the table and stood, fists clenched. "And you let your friend walk into possible death without a care?"

"We did not worry." Lailani shook her head beseechingly. "Why do you think we told her to hire you?"

SIX

The silence from her side of the car was deafening.
She was pissed...and crying. Riley tried to
ignore Di's sniffles. She was tough enough that he figured
she wouldn't want him mentioning her tears. But they got
to him.

Big time.

Especially the tears of a fairly confident, competent
woman like Di. The urge to pull her into his arms and offer
her comfort nagged at him, until he knew he had to do
something or he would give in to the urge to offer physical
consolation. And it was neither the time or the place.

"You okay?" He took his attention off the road long
enough to gauge her response.

"I'm fine," she answered but it was watery. Too watery.
"Except for the fact that you had another agenda."

Okay. He hadn't figured she'd learn of his secondary
mission but it was too late to hide it now. The reality was
that her friends had put her into a dangerous situation and
he was more equipped than someone without his training to
get her out of this mess.

"My primary objective is to keep you safe." But Riley couldn't lie. The intelligence that they'd given him was golden. Because he was pretty sure the prevailing thought in the U.S. was that if anyone broke the treaty it would be the more radical factions of MNLF. So assuming that her friends were telling the truth, the U.S. government needed to understand that the true threat to peace was a faction of the Philippine military. Not the members of MNLF or the other rebel groups.

And if that faction knew that Riley and Di had that information, and that Riley had the connections to relay it to the U.S. government, they were dead.

Shit. It all circled back to her friends. "Shouldn't you be pissed at your friends?"

He was still angry that they'd put Di in danger.

"She tried to stop me from coming with the supplies."

"Wait. What?" Riley continued to scan the road. They had at least an hour before they were back in Jolo. He likely wouldn't rest until they were on the plane back to the States tomorrow. Nothing like being in country with a military target on your back.

"I ignored her. I wanted to come home."

"Home?"

"I told you I grew up here." Di swallowed down a sob.

She'd stopped crying. And she wasn't yelling at him. Which he'd like to avoid. Distraction was the key to diffusing her anguish and her anger. Riley was pretty sure if he could get her talking she'd forget she was pissed at him.

"So what made you start Tools for Schools?"

"Books, school were a place of safety when I was a kid." She wiped away the tears from her cheeks. "We didn't have much."

Based on his knowledge of the island's history, he knew

that when she was growing up that the entire island was a haven for terrorists of many persuasions. Definitely not a calm, peaceful environment. It was only in the last twelve years that with the U.S. government and corporate sponsors that the day to day violence had tapered off.

Riley waited patiently, knowing she wasn't done.

"Then when I was fourteen, my parents sent me back to the States to boarding school."

She was quiet. So quiet, that he chanced another look at her. But her gaze was focused far away in the past. "I hated it. Everything was different. Bigger, louder, more chaotic. I didn't fit anywhere since I'd spent my childhood in a rural island culture. And I missed my friends. But I found my way with books. I buried myself in books. Found new worlds. Found myself."

Books. His nemesis. Her saviors.

"But my friends here weren't as lucky," Di said quietly. "So I started collecting leftover books, mostly for teens and I would mail them to my friends. When I finished a book I would send it along. If the library was cleaning out their stacks, I'd send those."

Riley admired her for thinking about her friends at such a normally self-absorbed age.

"But soon it got to be too expensive, because the boxes were heavy. So I solicited donations to pay for the shipping."

"So your activism roots started early." He glanced at her and smiled a warm, real smile.

She smiled back, her face lit with genuine understanding. "Yep."

"That's great."

"Then I went away to college. But I kept sending books whenever I could. And then my friends started asking for their younger siblings, or their cousins, or now, their kids. And boy is that weird."

Riley shuddered. He couldn't even imagine.

"So after college I used my business degree and I set up Tools for Schools."

"That's great." And he meant it. What a fantastic way to give back to the place that had nurtured her through her childhood.

"Thanks." She smiled tremulously.

They were just passing through the area that worried him the most so he turned his attention to their surroundings. "Keep a lookout for anything out of the ordinary or unusual."

"Why?"

"According to my intel and Magtanggol, this is the most dangerous pass we have to traverse right here."

Riley was worried. There were so many variables at play. If anyone from their little band leaked their route back to Jolo they were dead. If the military decided to send out multiple convoys, instead of just following the route Riley had given the truck rental place, they were dead. If the MNLF were wrong about the military's plans, they were dead.

He really didn't like how much dead kept popping up in his vocabulary right now. "I need you to be hyper-vigilant."

"I got that." Di propped her chin on her fist and kept a lookout.

The temptation to rev the engine and get the hell out of here was strong. But for one, the car that her friends had given them for the trip back likely wouldn't go much more than thirty-five. Any car in this area wasn't going to move fast. To blend in, they needed to maintain their cover speed.

The tension in the car rose as they slowly puttered along.

And Riley's feeling of unease grew. Riley heaved a silent sigh and willed the hard knot of tension to loosen. "About another hour." Maybe a little more if the rain kept up.

Riley scanned their surroundings. Then he noted the deep furrows on the side of the road. Furrows likely made by heavy truck tires as in military trucks. Shit. That wasn't a good sign.

He glanced in the rear view mirror, looking for any other signs of soldiers or heavy trucks. But he didn't see any.

"I have a bad feeling about this." He handed her the extra weapon. "Be ready."

Di nodded, her face reflected the same unease that was pulling at his gut.

And then Riley heard the rumble of heavy trucks over the light rain. Trucks plural. Shit this could not be good.

"We need to bail." Riley quickly pulled the car as far off the road and into the brush and vegetation as possible, turned off the engine, and hoped that the indeterminate color would be hidden by the rain and bushes.

Not to mention that there were enough abandoned cars along the roadsides on Jolo that hopefully whoever was in the trucks would take note but not stop. If they touched the hood of the car they would know that it had been recently driven.

But they should be looking for the delivery truck. Not this old sedan.

"What?"

"Now."

"But—"

"Not the time to argue." He grabbed his backpack from the back seat, shoved open the driver's door. "Trust me."

Thankfully she shut her mouth and sprang into action.

They exited the car at the same time and slammed their

doors shut. Riley hustled around the front of the car, grabbed Di's hand, and tugged her into the overgrown cover of the jungle just as a convoy of trucks came from the direction of Jolo city. They shouldn't even be on this road. Dammit.

Riley pulled Di behind the trunk of a Narra tree and pressed her back against the wide trunk. Fortunately their clothing should blend right into nature's color palette. He leaned into her, pressed her head into his neck, surrounded her. If he could absorb her into his skin so that no one would notice her, he would.

"You understand that if they find us. They will kill us and blame your friends." Riley said softly into her ear, "It's a lose-lose for us and them."

"More for us," she said drily.

Riley held his weapon down by his leg but realistically he knew that his one weapon against a truckload of well-armed soldiers was worthless. Di's heart beat so hard he could feel the tremble of her breasts. And if he wasn't so worried about the possibility of discovery he'd be enjoying the way Di was pressed up against him, her body closer to his than ever before.

The trucks, two of them, lumbered along the muddy road. Riley could see two rows of soldiers, lined up on benches in the back, sixteen or so per truck.

He rested his forehead on Di's shoulder and swore softly. There was no way he could hold off thirty-two men. He had to pray that they kept driving. The first truck slowed. "Fuck," he gritted out softly.

Di's body tensed beneath his. "What's wrong?" she whispered.

"They're slowing."

The driver peered through the windshield at the car. He

called out something indistinguishable to the soldiers behind them, then lifted a piece of paper to his face. Riley had never prayed harder in his life. Hopefully they were looking for the truck.

"Drive on by," Riley muttered. For fuck's sake.

"These aren't the droids you're looking for." Di's lips moved against his neck.

He wanted to laugh. Instead he kept his gaze trained on the soldiers. And tried to come up with anything he could do to protect Di if they got out and came to investigate the car.

Finally the driver shook his head. One of the guys in back lifted a two-way radio to his mouth and began to speak. The driver of the second truck gave the first driver a thumbs up.

"Don't move." He nuzzled the skin of her neck. "Looks like they're driving on by, but we need to stay perfectly still, in case anyone is watching the jungle."

"Okay," she said breathlessly.

The soldiers in the back of the trucks continued to scan the vegetation. Riley prayed to every God he'd ever heard of that he and Di hadn't left any major tracks that they soldiers could see. Their exit from the car and into the trees hadn't exactly been stealthy.

Di held her breath as they waited for the trucks to pass.

Finally the trucks disappeared around the bend in the road. And still Riley didn't move. But he was suddenly far more aware of the world around them. Rain dripped from the canopy above, and slid down the back of his neck, his clothes were soaked. The supple strength of Di's body heated his front, her nipples were hard buttons against his pecs, and her breath was hot against the shell of his ear.

Monkeys chattered in the tree tops, frogs croaked, and

birds clicked and clacked. Steam rose from the jungle floor bathing the entire area in a soft, white mist as the rain trailed off.

And still he waited.

"Can we move yet?" But there was no sense of urgency to her question, and her body had softened and melted against his.

"Not yet," Riley said. "We need to wait, make sure they don't double back."

"Do you really think they will?" Di asked doubtfully.

"I refuse to let anything happen to you."

Riley's mind was moving at Mach speed as he flipped through different possible scenarios. If they were lucky, the soldiers would assume they would stick to their plan. The one that even Riley had thought they'd be following and they'd given to the truck owner. Di's deception may have just saved them. If her friends came through, then the soldiers should continue up that hill and into the mountains.

"Do you think Lailani and Magtanggol will be okay?"

"If the soldiers follow our originally planned route, your friends will be fine." Riley nuzzled the delicate skin beneath Di's ear. "They should get back to their *sitio* before the soldiers intersect with the original route we filed."

Damn he wished they still had the SAT phone. But they'd gotten rid of it just in case the military had the radar to track them if they used it. He'd hated to leave it behind but no one could get here to help them and the chance that the military could find them if they used it convinced Riley to leave it.

"Can we get back in the car soon?" Di asked. Her hands had come up to hold onto Riley, fingers fisted in the belt loops at his sides and her hips canted toward his.

His cock, which had been at half mast, surged to life at her surrounding heat.

Adrenaline had dumped into his system at the danger when he'd heard the trucks. The chemical now morphed into raging desire. Desire he couldn't assuage here and now, dammit.

But they could have a little fun until they needed to move.

Riley kissed a slow path down the side of her neck and nudged aside the collar of her cotton shirt to press soft, sucking kisses against her delicate collarbone.

Di was pulling his shirt from his combat pants, her palm hot and smooth against his back, when he heard the tell-tale rumble. Fuck.

"They're coming back." Riley jerked away from her. "Let's go."

"Go where?" She tugged at her hand ineffectually.

"In there." Riley nodded toward the jungle. "Quickly."

Di's eyes widened but she nodded, and they took off.

HOURS LATER, Di sagged against the trunk of a Narra tree. Every bone and muscle in her body was sore and aching. And all she'd done was follow in Riley's footsteps. Once they'd ventured further into the jungle and could no longer see the road, Riley took a wicked-looking machete from his pack and started swinging to clear a path.

He'd stop and consult his watch, then adjust their direction, so minutely that it didn't seem to her that it would make much difference, but he seemed to think it would.

Gone was the suave, charming guy. Several hours in the jungle, and he was stripped of that veneer. Instead, Riley was pure primal male. The stubble on his face should have softened the line of his jaw, instead he seemed more hard angles and uncompromising strength. His arm muscles rippled with exertion as he swung the machete through the vegetation. Sweat blotched his t-shirt and sheened his body. Every line screamed predator, and protector. His face was feral and fierce. And she had no doubt that he would defend her with his life.

Darkness would fall soon. And she was woman enough to admit that the idea of spending the night in the open, such as it was, jungle was terrifying. She'd managed to put all the bugs and snakes out of her mind while they were moving. But now that they'd stopped, every swish and rustle of the leaves made her wonder what was beneath them or crawling on the trees and ferns.

So far they hadn't seen any snakes, but honestly she hadn't been looking too hard.

Riley had mustered on, stopping when she needed to rest, never judging, never complaining. From the bowels of his never-ending backpack, he'd pulled out a water bottle and some purifying tablets.

He glanced at his watch, then looked up. The sky was a gray blur above the thick canopy of trees. "We're going to need to stop."

"Stop?!" Di protested. "Shouldn't we keep going?" Even she could hear the panic in her voice.

"Di." Riley laid a comforting hand on her shoulder, but even the reassuring weight of his capable palm couldn't quite calm her. "We'll be okay."

Riley swung his backpack off his shoulders, and then unzipped the main pocket. With a wicked smile, he pulled out what looked like a thin nylon and mesh rectangle. "Shelter."

"What is it?"

"A tent." With economical movements, he set up the very small tent. It was going to be a tight fit.

Riley nodded to the tree she'd been leaning against. "Best go to the little girls' room on the other side of that tree. I don't want you wandering off."

Di snorted. As if.

By the time she took care of business, Riley had the tent completely set up. He'd pulled two MRE'S, ready to eat meals, from another pouch in his magic backpack . He handed one to Di and opened his own and sucked it down.

"How did you—"

"Preparation." Riley grinned. His face had a slash of dirt across one cheekbone and his short dark hair was mussed, but his hazel eyes glowed with amusement. "I only have enough for a day."

"But you still thought to bring this with us." He couldn't possibly have predicted the events of the last few hours and yet, he'd still managed to have the right supplies.

"That's what you pay me for."

Thank goodness she'd chosen GHR. Except, she hadn't really. Betrayal burned in her breast. Lailani should have known better than to put her in danger. What if she'd chosen some other company to bring the school supplies to Jolo? What if Riley hadn't been as competent as they'd believed? Di would likely be dead. Or worse.

"Look. Most of our deliveries were within a day or two walk from the main city." Riley efficiently wrapped his trash in a plastic bag and stored it in another pocket of the magic backpack.

Emotion clogged her throat as she realized that he was more than a charming, pretty face. And thank goodness for that. "Thank you."

His teeth were a small flash in his face, but he didn't reply as they finished cleaning up from their dinner.

"After you." Riley bowed as if he were dressed in a formal tux and she in an evening gown. And Di wanted to giggle. But she wasn't a giggler. Ever. So what the hell kind of spell had he cast over her?

She slid into the very small tent. "This is going to be a—"

"Tight fit." Riley's voice was low and full of promise.

Di shivered as his husky voice rasped over her nerve endings. She shimmied into the tent and then she started to shiver in earnest, but not from his sexy voice.

She was wet and cold.

Di began to take off her boots. She could feel Riley behind her, and as soon as he zipped the tent completely closed the interior began to heat up. But Di was still shaking hard as she removed her damp socks.

She was thinking about the night to come, and about trying to resist his charms, until he said, "You need to take everything off."

SEVEN

"Excuse me?" Di's voice was snippy, her back stiff with disapproval.

Riley knew the only way to overcome her resistance to taking off her clothes was to piss her off even more. He had to get her out of those wet clothes.

"Come on, sweetheart, don't be a prude," he drawled. The anger would heat her up too.

She plopped down on the 'floor'. "While your request was charming," she sneered. "I don't think so."

Riley leaned forward and whispered in her ear, "You've got to take it off, or you'll get hypothermia."

"We're in the jungle," she scoffed.

"But it cools off at night and your clothes are damp. What's wrong, don't you trust yourself around me?"

That did it. As Riley thought it might. She ripped her tan Henley over her head and he could make out the sinuous line of her back in the fading light. Ry swallowed when he saw her pale blue lace bra.

"Where are we going to dry them?" She shimmied out

of her cargo pants and he nearly groaned at the matching thong panties. Of course a woman as down to earth as Di, who dressed straight out of an REI catalog, wore barely there lace underwear that revealed her absolutely stunning ass.

"We'll lay the clothes out underneath us." Riley pulled his camouflage shirt over his head, his words muffled as he continued. "We've got two Mylar survival blankets. We'll put one on top of the clothes, and then the other on top of us."

Riley awkwardly removed his boots and pants. Heated skin, floral perfume, and ozone after a hard rain scented the air in the tiny tent.

This was going to be hell.

Riley hadn't done it on purpose. On the other hand, he was looking forward to holding her in his arms.

He carefully laid the clothes out, then lay the first blanket over their damp clothes. Then he opened the second blanket. "Lie down."

Di said, "We're going to bed now?"

"Unless you've got a better idea." The amusement in his voice was clear.

She harrumphed and then spread out.

Riley lay down behind her and pulled the blanket over their cool bodies. Di shivered again. "Don't hit me," he said. "But we need to get you warm."

Her teeth began to chatter. "Ok-okay."

Riley spooned up against her back and legs, then curled his arm around her waist and pulled her snug to his body. He tried not to think about the fact that the only barrier between the naked skin of her ass was his cotton boxer briefs. Her whole body shook as he tried to rub some warmth into her skin.

"God, your skin is soft," he whispered as her shivering began to abate.

"Yours is hot," she stuttered.

He rubbed his hands over her skin. She was finally starting to warm up. Riley scooted his groin away from the curve of her butt as the proximity of their bodies began to impact his. But before he could ease even further away, she instinctively edged back to connect skin to skin as many places as she could, her body seeking the heat of his.

"Oh." In her attempts to get warm, she'd managed to caress his fully stiff cock with her butt.

Riley cleared his throat. "Sorry." But he wasn't. He was a normal, healthy male with a naked female body cuddled up against his. The fact that his body responded was completely natural.

Di tried to lay perfectly still. The warm male body behind her was a distraction, no question. He felt good. Better than good. Amazing. His body was usually hidden beneath clothes that fit but didn't necessarily emphasize his ripped muscles. He was an exquisite muscular work of art, with sleek biceps and a rippling eight pack. She'd nearly moaned aloud when he'd pulled his shirt over his head.

She blushed. Not that he could see it. Her heart picked up tempo, and arousal rushed to her sex. The man was sex on a stick and she was practically naked and pressed up against him. Her nipples peaked and her body responded to the attraction she'd been trying desperately to ignore. But suddenly ignoring the physical sensations pouring through her was impossible.

Riley rubbed her skin roughly trying to warm her up. But Di wasn't shivering from the cold anymore. She was responding to his rough hands sliding up and down her arms and the persistent throb of his erection against her ass.

Was his breath coming faster? She felt the hot puff against the back of her neck and her pulse quickened. Di held her breath, wishing, hoping he'd make a move.

She wouldn't stop him.

She knew with the very core of her being that sex with him would be amazing. Fantastic. An out-of-body experience. And after this crazy day and his confession, she wanted him more than ever. She wanted the experience of Riley Stone sliding hot and hard into her body.

But Riley only continued to rub her skin, without any sexual undertones. He was trying to impersonally warm her up. While they were almost naked. It was enough to make a lesser girl cringe.

What the hell was she doing, waiting for him to make a move?

She was no coward. She'd learned a long time ago to go after what she wanted. And she wanted Riley Stone.

Di took a deep breath and rolled around quickly so they were face to face. Riley jerked back in surprise, his face an impassive mask. Di didn't give him time to say anything. She pressed her mouth to his and ran her hands down his hard body.

For an instant, he froze. Not even his mouth moved beneath hers. Her breasts rubbed against his chest as she wrapped her arms around his muscled torso and slid her leg between his muscled thighs. The hot spear of his erection throbbed against the sensitive skin of her stomach. But he still hadn't moved.

Di's influx of confidence began to fade. Maybe she'd read the signals wrong. Maybe he turned that sexual charm on everyone whether he was interested or not.

The thought hadn't even cleared her brain when Riley burst into action. And they combusted. He cupped her face in his large hands, slanted his head and devoured her mouth. While he attacked her mouth, he rolled her onto her back and then over on top of her. His heavy weight anchored her to the Mylar blanket beneath them, and she ran her hands along the muscled smoothness of his back and down to his ass.

Riley dragged his tongue down her neck and her body tingled. He nipped at her collarbone and pressed wet, open-mouthed kisses along her shoulder while his hands explored her body.

He skimmed his fingertips across her chest and her nipples tightened into hard painful peaks, but he didn't touch. Instead he smoothed his hand along her arm, until his palm slid against hers and he laced their fingers together and stopped long enough to press a sweet kiss to her knuckles.

She clamped her arm around his neck and pulled him in closer. She twined her body around his like the orchids that sinuously wrapped around the trunks of the tropical trees.

Riley rocked his hips into hers, the hard blade of his erection rubbed her clit and everything in her clenched, then softened. He ate at her mouth like a man starving.

All thoughts that he wasn't interested flew away in an instant. This was not the practiced seduction of a player. Instead he touched her as if he were ravenous for a taste, as if he'd couldn't stand to be separated from her for even an instant.

She moaned softly in the private cocoon of the little tent and trembled from the sensations bombarding her. Riley rocked into her, once, twice, then groaned long and hard. He tore his mouth from hers.

His hair was mussed and sticking straight up from her

fingers as his chest heaved and his cock throbbed against her clit. She was so close. Which is why at first his words didn't register.

"We have to stop."

Finally his meaning penetrated. Stop? Was he out of his mind?

He was propped up above her, his arms flexed as he supported his body, hovering over top of her.

"What?"

"Do you have any condoms?" he asked.

"I get a quarterly shot," she said desperately. Which she did.

Riley pushed all the way off her and rolled to his back. His cock tented his underwear and looked to be painful.

"I won't put you at risk." Riley threw his forearm over his eyes and groaned as if in pain.

"You have a disease I should know about?"

Riley snorted. "Of course not."

"And you don't have any condoms with you?"

"No. Dammit," Riley snarled.

But her heart sank as she realized that this wasn't about condoms, this was about him and her and about them together.

"So you're refusing to have sex with me." Di enunciated each word clearly, wanting his rejection to be absolutely clear. Di crossed her arms over her chest, trying unobtrusively to cover her body. Her physical nakedness was no match for her emotional one, she felt rejected, exposed.

But that humiliation turned to anger. Rage bubbled in her stomach and roiled through her body. Even under threat and running from danger, he couldn't be bothered to have sex with her.

"I think refusing is the wrong word." Riley gutted out, "Postponing, would be better."

"You think you're going to charm your way out of this?" she snarled. "With everything that's happened over the last few days and the threat of the military finding us, I'm not good enough to bang?"

No way was she going to let him get away with trying to charm her out of embarrassment. She was going to make him face up to his rejection.

Riley yanked her on top of him, and she stared down into his angular, handsome face, covered with the day's stubble and a smudge of dirt. He looked primal, and angry. What the hell did he have to be angry about? He was the one refusing her.

"Look. I have rules. And number one on my list is: No sex without double protection. Ever. It's a rule I refuse to break."

"Right." Sarcasm was her refuge.

"I am not going to end up like my father, with a bunch of kids running around that he didn't want." Riley's eyes darkened with residual pain. "I will not be like him," he said fiercely.

At first she thought he was still handing her a line. After all, he was good at them. Charm, cajole, sweet talk. But as she looked into his desperate hazel gaze, she saw the remnants of childhood pain.

"Oh, Riley." Di finally understood that he wasn't rejecting her. He was rejecting the situation. "Postponing, huh?"

"Yeah."

"I really do get a quarterly shot," she said softly.

"Con's mother was on the pill. Apparently dear old dad had power sperm," Riley snarked. "I take after him in a lot of ways. What if that's one of them? I won't leave you vulnerable to an unexpected pregnancy. It's double contracepation, double protection, or nothing."

And with that her heart melted again.

"Don't doubt that I want you." He nudged his hips upward, then gripped her waist and lifted her until her breasts were even with his mouth. He slid his palms along her sides and up until he was cupping her breasts in his hands. His thumbs brushed her nipples over and over, and he stared at his hands on her body as if fascinated by the contrast of his muscular wrists and long fingers on her paler, more delicate skin. His hot tongue traced the edge of her lace bra over the mounds of her breasts and then without warning he sucked her nipple into his mouth. Hard.

The hot pull of his mouth hit her sex like a punch. She gripped his shoulders in her palms and offered her breasts for his worship.

Di let her head fall forward, her hot, pulsing sex rested on Riley's straining abs, as she kissed him. She kissed his forehead, kissed across his face, and over to his ear. She sucked the sensitive skin of his earlobe into her mouth mimicking his pulls on her breasts, the sensation sizzled along her nerve endings and lust burst inside.

In an incredibly athletic move, Riley lifted her over his head, his mouth and teeth trailed a path over her stomach. Good God, he was strong. Then he pushed her up until his mouth could reach her mound and she straddled his face.

Riley pressed an open-mouthed kiss over her clit before he dragged her silk panties down with his thumbs and exposed her to his intimate kiss. The light in the quiet tent was nearly gone highlighting all of her other senses.

The scents of her musk and his arousal were thick in the murky air of the tent. Inside the shadowy cocoon, rain pattered on the waterproof ceiling and drowned out the other sounds of the jungle, entwining them in a thick intimate bubble.

She knew she should probably stop him, but she was drowning in sensation. Her body was one big sexual nerve as he brought her to a fever pitch of arousal. Every muscle trembled at the expert way he strummed her higher. Her sex clenched, begging for a thicker, harder penetration than the silken thrust of his tongue.

Riley didn't want Di to think that he didn't want her and he refused to put her at risk. However he could show her how much he craved her.

Her skin tasted of a hint of salt and the sweet perfume of her arousal made him dizzy with want. "I'm going to lick you right up," he growled against her sex.

Riley buried his nose in her curls and inhaled. "You smell divine." He sucked the button of her clit into his mouth and curled his tongue around the engorged bud.

Every moan he pulled from her was a triumph. He explored her sex, licking the slick folds. Then he thrust his tongue inside her channel, and pulled her down until she was grinding against his face. The sounds she was making while he feasted on her were driving him higher and higher. He was going to have the biggest case of blue balls in the history of mankind but he didn't care as long as he sent her over the edge into satisfaction.

Riley spread his fingers wide over the generous curve of her ass and rocked her against his face. He nipped her clit then ferociously ate at her sex until she let go with an involuntary groan. He continued to lick and suck her clit, reveling in the throb of her sex against his mouth.

The tension that had suffused her body blast away with

the force of her orgasm, and Riley rejoiced as she collapsed boneless against his face.

He pressed a sweet kiss to her sex and she shuddered as phantom ripples of desire feathered over her skin and her breath heaved in her chest. Her thighs trembled from the sensual explosion.

Riley blew a puff of breath against her quivering sex and smiled as she jerked from the barely there contact.

His dick was harder than the barrel of his gun. But he didn't care in the slightest.

"Let me." She started to slide down his body.

Di had just come harder than she'd ever come in her life. Her body was suffused with endorphins and the fervent wish to repay him in kind.

The tent had grown so dark that she couldn't even see her hand in front of her face. She pushed up to her knees and slid her hand down to the elastic waist of his tight boxer briefs. But Riley stopped her. "It's okay." His voice was deep, rough.

It wasn't okay. "But—"

He rationalized, "We don't have anything to clean up with."

She caressed his balls and he groaned again. She bowed over and kissed her way down Riley's face. She traced his features with her fingers, the arch of his eyebrow, the slight laugh lines that fanned out from his eyes, and only made him more appealing because it was clear he laughed alot. The high aristocratic cheekbones. She trailed her index finger along his nose and over the sensual curve of his lips.

He had a mouth made for kissing. She pressed a liquid, wet, kiss of gratitude to his mouth and tasted her own passion on his tongue. She sipped from him and made love to his mouth, and lost herself in the pleasure of pleasing him.

She could tell he was smiling as she kissed the curve of his mouth. She lay down along his side, and continued to kiss him in slow, sweet sensual abandon.

"What was that for?" he asked when she finally stopped.

"Because I could."

EIGHT

Riley's watch vibrated, buzz-buzz-buzz, against his wrist.

He came fully awake from his light sleep. Dawn was breaking. The light inside the very small tent was barely there and cast everything in a pale gray haze. Di's smooth skin and lean limbs were draped over his body as if they'd slept together for years rather than one night.

Her light brown lashes fanned against the angles of her cheekbones, and her mouth, that mouth that had kissed him so sweetly, was soft and curved in sleep. Her short blond hair lay on her forehead and curled against her cheek and jaw.

All her edges disappeared when she was relaxed and asleep. He loved her edges. The quick wit, the acerbic comments, the way she called him on his bullshit.

But this softer, sweeter Di was appealing too.

Riley let himself just lie there and watch her sleep for a bit. As the sun was coming up, Di started to wake and as consciousness came back to her he could see the edges take shape. Until she stretched, yawned wide and opened her pale, ice blue eyes.

"Rise and shine, honey," he drawled.

A deep flush worked over her body as her memory returned with her edges.

He thought for a minute that she wouldn't meet his gaze but not his Di. She resolutely lifted her chin and looked him straight in the eye. "Morning."

Hopefully their clothes weren't completely damp. The temperature in the island jungle was already rising. If they made good time, and avoided the military, they could still catch their flight out today.

He was pretty sure the soldiers hadn't followed them. They'd be searching for them and the truck on the roads. They wouldn't think to look in the jungle. And thanks to Lailani and Magtanggol they weren't anywhere near the roads. But that didn't mean they could relax. He wouldn't relax until they were in the air and off Jolo Island.

"We need to get gone." Riley executed a sit up with Di still half on top of him.

Her little hum of approval vibrated through him as he lifted her and set her to the side. Riley folded the Mylar blankets.

They put on their damp clothes, awkwardly bumping into each other in the tight confines of the little tent.

"Ugh." But Di was smiling as she pulled on her Henley. The damp fabric clung to her pert breasts. Riley's mouth watered. He couldn't wait to get his hands on her again. Once they were safe. And had protection.

"If we don't run into any trouble, we can likely make the airport in time to catch our flight."

"But—"

"We need to get off this island."

Before they left, he needed to write down as much

information about the soldiers and the other rebel factions on the island as he could detail.

Riley had already noted the lat and long of where the trucks came from and where they were likely headed. He noted the type of vehicle, the number of soldiers, their uniforms, and weapons by texting into his cell phone. But his thumbs were slow.

"What are you doing?"

"Notes," Riley said shortly as he laboriously entered the information.

"Do you...want some help?"

"Sure." He handed her his cell. He dictated all the information he could think of while he broke down the tent. She entered the data in the phone far more quickly than he could.

After he was done speaking, Di kept typing.

"What are you doing?"

"Adding to your notes."

Riley raised his eyebrows. "Thanks."

"Too bad we can't just call someone for a pick up." She joked as she finished entering the information in his cell.

"Yeah." Unfortunately the cell was useless in the jungle. Even if there was someone they could safely call. "Let's get moving. The sooner we get out of here, the happier I'll be."

Riley checked the coordinates on his watch and turned in the proper direction. That was when he realized what time it was.

Dammit. He'd missed his check-in with Jack.

Hopefully once they arrived back in Jolo he'd have time to make a call. It was first time he'd missed check-in. He actually had a few days before the company hit def-con one and came looking for them. And Riley knew that Jack had confidence in him and his ability to get the job done. So he shrugged and didn't worry too much.

"Let's hit it."

THEY LANDED in San Francisco almost twenty hours after getting on the plane in Jolo by the skin of their teeth.

"It is now safe to use your portable electronic devices. Please refrain from leaving your seat until the plane has stopped at the gate."

Nanette, their first class flight attendant, made a point to stop by Riley's seat. "It was a pleasure serving you today, Riley." She practically purred the words, her mouth pursed and slicked with a new layer of glossy red lipstick as she rested her fingers on his wrist. "Please let me know if you need anything else."

Beside him, Di stiffened. He could practically hear Di rolling her eyes at Nan's barely veiled come-on.

"Thanks, Nan." He kept his tone and smile light as he gently brushed off the unspoken offer. "Nice to see you again."

He and Nanette had hooked up last year after they'd met on the exact same Manila to SFO flight. And he knew that with one suggestive smile and his Platinum Amex, they could be ensconced in a suite at the Westin about twenty minutes after clearing customs and within thirty he could be inside her.

But Riley didn't want easy or flirty. He wanted the prickly, contrary, compassionate, silent woman on his right.

The gleam in Nanette's eyes faded as she realized that Riley had no intention of a repeat of the last time they'd seen each other.

It wasn't his fault he happened to know the flight attendant. From Di's seat, the flight back had been filled with a condemning silence. She'd avoided talking to him for the long flight home by sleeping, or pretending to sleep, when he was awake. And he'd finally crashed about eight hours into the flight.

Now Di hustled ahead of him, barreling through the customs line with the focus of an Indy car driver on the straightaway to the checkered flag.

Customs wouldn't take her long. They hadn't gone back to their hotel in Jolo to get their bags. Riley wanted to avoid any possibility of being picked up by the Philippine military faction who was against the peace accord. He had known once they got to the relative safety of the Jolo Airport they would be okay.

Riley had ditched the knives and machete just before they hit the ornately-tiled arch to the Jolo Airport, but he had brought his other weapons home with him. So, for him, customs was going to be a little more involved. He unzipped his pack, whipped out his permits, and kept a tight eye on Di's progress through the re-entry line.

Fortunately, she got held up at a slow moving customs counter, and he managed to speed through his own line so they finished at about the same time. Riley could see her heading for the parking garage. But he knew she didn't have the keys to her car. They'd been left behind in the hotel.

"Di, wait up."

She was practically running. He strode purposefully toward her and when he got close enough, he grabbed her bicep. She jerked to a stop so quickly that he almost ran into her. "How are you getting home?"

He really wanted to ask where home was. He didn't even know where she lived.

"I'll get a ride." She pasted a totally fake smile on her lips and stared over his right shoulder.

It had only been seven days since they had left California. He definitely hadn't thought they'd become besties during the trip but her frigid answer after their adventure in the jungle was pissing him off. "I'll take you home."

"That's not necessary."

"All part of the GHR package." Riley let his company smile come out.

Her pale blue eyes narrowed, and her mouth pursed. She didn't like it when he was his usual charming self. "Really. Not necessary."

He held onto her arm in a tight but not hurtful grip. "I insist." Riley said, "After all, we need to discuss the trip and what went right and what went wrong. GHR takes customer service very seriously."

Which was bullshit, but damned if he'd let her leave him.

She wanted to call him on his lie. He could tell by every line in her body, but she finally nodded reluctantly. "Okay, fine."

"Great." He grinned at her. He was inordinately happy to get her in his clutches again. Riley lead her to long-term parking and his car. His brothers had more modern fast cars but Riley preferred his old-fashioned muscle car. The 1967 Pontiac GTO with custom leather seats and a 400 HO engine was a classic.

Fortunately, he'd carried his car keys in his emergency backpack—along with their passports, so they'd been able to get on the plane without any problems—so he had the means to get home. Otherwise, he'd have had to call one of his brothers to bring him the spare set.

When he lead Di to his car she merely raised an eyebrow and slid in the passenger seat. He knew she was re-thinking her interest in him. Perversely, her feigned indifference was hitting every single hot button he didn't know he had. He'd be damned if now that they were back in the States she blew him off.

Riley knew all about opportunities and regrets. And while he was still on board with them getting together he'd been re-thinking things too. Riley's Rules Number Eight: Never get involved with a client. He knew it was a very bad idea. But he'd likely jump if she asked how high.

Riley threw his backpack in the trunk and then got behind the wheel.

Di avoided him by scrolling through information on her cell phone.

"We need to talk about it," Riley said as he fired up the super-charged engine. She was clearly still pissed about Nanette's obvious come-on. But it wasn't like he'd encouraged her.

"No we don't." She rolled toward the passenger door and curled into a tight ball. She might be blocking him out right this minute, but he wasn't going to let this lie.

"Nan and I had a thing—"

"Wake me when we get to Monterey." She fake yawned and effectively shut him down.

Dammit. Riley slammed his palms against the steering wheel. He wanted to push but she really did look exhausted. Her face was pale and the delicate skin beneath her ice blue, blank eyes was bruised. "Fine. We'll talk later."

Within minutes, Di was asleep.

Riley had tried to call Jack during their very quick layover in Manila but Jack hadn't answered, which was beyond unusual. Jack always answered his cell. Riley was antsy to get back to the office and Monterey and figure out what was going on. In the meantime, he'd left a long message for Jack that didn't get into specifics but let his big brother know that he had critical information for their client.

Since he hadn't been able to touch base with Jack from the Philippines, Riley called Jack again while he navigated the road home. But Jack didn't answer the office phone or his cell. Again. What the hell?

Riley frowned. He checked his cell in case he had a missed call or text. Connor had called him, several times a day, since he'd missed check in.

Weird.

Riley pressed speed dial and Con answered his cell immediately. "You okay?"

"Yeah. We're fine." Riley raised his eyebrows. Con sounded the tiniest bit worried.

"Where are you?"

"On 101 just south of Gilroy."

"You're back in the States?" Con burst out. "Jesus, Riley, you didn't think to call?"

"I called Jack." Riley glanced over at Di but she was still sound asleep. "What's wrong ?"

Connor sounded like he'd taken a Jack pill. All worried and uptight.

"You missed check in. Twice."

"We had a bit of a situation," Riley understated. "And then I didn't have time to call before we took off. I left Jack a message."

"Yeah, well, Jack is basically MIA." Con sighed. "And so were you. Ava, Jess, and I were...concerned."

Was it his imagination or was there an emphasis on Ava

and Connor? When did they get together? And since when did Connor and Jess even communicate with each other?

He'd only been out of the country for seven days, and out of touch for two. "Feeling a little like I went down the rabbit hole here, Con."

"You have no idea." Connor said, "Jack left a few days ago and we weren't able to get ahold of him. You were gone and not checking in. Ava was attacked. The company computers survived an attempted hack."

"Ava okay?" Riley pressed the pedal harder. He needed to get home. It sounded like all hell was breaking loose.

"Yeah. Long story." But there was an easy smile in Con's voice that Riley hadn't heard in...ever.

"Tell it to me when I get there."

"Will do." Con asked, "You okay? Client okay?"

"Yeah." Riley glanced over at Di who was softly snoring. "Getting there."

"Ry?"

"Yeah?"

"Glad you're home safe and sound."

"Thanks, bro." Riley swallowed. "See you soon."

Riley glanced at her, noting her filthy pants. Riley had given her the one clean white t-shirt he'd carried in his pack. And he couldn't stop the visceral thrill of seeing her in his oversized shirt. It was sophomoric and he didn't care.

He tried to ignore the ripe smell coming from his own clothes. They hadn't had time to do more than clean off with baby wipes, and slather on deodorant at the airport in Manila.

He shrugged and continued driving toward Monterey. She'd let him know where she lived when they got closer.

But as Riley motored down Highway 101, he realized if

he let her go, even home to regroup, they'd never get back to where they'd been in that tent.

And he knew what he had to do. He wasn't taking her home.

NINE

The sudden quiet woke Di. Disoriented, she blinked her eyes open and glanced around the strange car's interior. She quickly flashed through the last day and half, and remembered Riley insisted on giving her a ride home. But she wasn't home. She was in Riley's car which was no longer moving. Where the hell were they?

Di glanced around and finally recognized the underground parking garage of GHR's building. The distinctly American structure and sounds from the street above were harsh noise after the more natural sounds from the jungles and beaches of Jolo Island. She already missed the familiar scents and sounds of her childhood home.

Di stretched her arms above her head and yawned. She leaned her head back against the headrest and her head lolled to the side. She finally realized that Riley was getting their stuff from the trunk of his classic car.

"I don't live here," she said to him as he crouched down on the passenger side and rested his elbows on the open window frame.

"I know." He gave her that smile. The one he'd tried to

use on her in the office the very first time they met. She'd kind of been hoping that Riley wouldn't make an appearance. But of course, he did. That Riley was the one who picked up flight attendants. And with that thought her temper started to simmer. Mostly at herself. She was the one stupid enough to think their encounter in the jungle had been the start of something. Stupid.

"Let's go on up to the office."

"I don't want to go to the office," she said politely through gritted teeth. "I want to go home."

"We just have one last **GHR** detail to go over and then I'll take you home."

She didn't trust him. His smile had an edge that hadn't been there before. What was he up to?

"I can just call a cab," she countered. "I don't live too far from here."

Di needed to get away from him. Now that they were back in the real world, she needed to get over this strange attraction that Riley Stone held for her. He was a player. She may have forgotten for a few insane moments in the jungle, but now she remembered. And she knew that the last thing she needed was to get involved with a guy like him. Even for a night.

She never thought she'd be grateful that he had rules but right now she was thanking the fates that they hadn't had any condoms.

She needed to retreat back into her comfortable head space and chalk up that last day in the jungle to some sort of fear-induced aberrant behavior. Riley Stone couldn't possibly be as sweet as she'd believed. Couldn't possibly be as into her as she'd assumed. She must have romanticized him while they were fighting their way back to civilization.

"Not yet, honey." He gripped his backpack, and her cell phone in his large, capable fist.

"Are you—are you holding me hostage?"

Riley laughed. The sound was rich, warm and very amused.

"Of course not." But then he turned on his heel and headed for the building's elevator, completely ignoring her wishes. "Come on."

Di saw red. Who the hell did he think he was?

She stomped toward him and hopped into the elevator, just as the doors were closing on her. "Give me my cell." She snatched at her smart phone but he held it above his head and slightly behind him so the only way she'd be able to reach it was if she pressed him flat against the elevator wall and plastered her body against his.

He raised an arched brow at her and smirked. *Go for it, honey.*

"Are you really that desperate?"

"You wanna press the button for the fourth floor?"

She wanted to bash him upside the head. Di clenched her fists, and took control of her temper. Then pressed the damn button.

They rode the elevator in silence. Once they got to the door to GHR, Riley extracted his office keys from the backpack and opened the door.

He bowed and extended his arm. "After you."

Di snorted. And the inelegant sound made him smile. He was tired. He still had to file his top-secret report. And he needed to talk to her, had to make her see reason. See him.

Riley unlocked the door to Jack's office and flipped on the lights. His palms were damp as he gestured to the chair across from Jack's desk. "Have a seat."

He thought about the first time he'd seen her sitting in that very chair. He'd walked into this room and something about her nearly brought him to his knees. But he knew now that she was immune to his charm. Immune to the one trait that defined him.

So why in the hell did he even want to pursue this?

Di threw herself into the black leather chair, while Riley sat down at Jack's desk. A sheaf of papers lay scattered on the floor underneath the desk. He frowned. Why would there be papers *under* the desk? He glanced across the cordovan leather blotter and noticed that Jack's fancy pen and holder were askew and the picture of the four siblings had fallen face down on the desktop. "What happened here?" he wondered aloud.

"Can we get through this?" Di sniped. "So I can go home and crash. This is ridiculous. It's like you want me to be pissed at you."

Riley hated the distance between them. Why had he ever thought that having the desk between them would lend credence to his words? She was mentally backing away with every word he uttered. And that was unacceptable.

He didn't want her to go to her home. What he wanted was for her to go home with him and crash in *his* bed. And instead of finesse, he just blurted out, "Come home with me."

Di blinked. Her pale brown lashes fanned across her high cheekbones and then lifted. "What?"

"Come home with me."

"You're out of your mind." She stood abruptly. "I don't know what kind of game you're playing, but you need to stop. Right now."

Riley thought he'd lost. But then he watched her pulse flutter in the base of her throat. She was nervous.

Riley moved around the desk to stop her from leaving. "I have condoms there," he said bluntly. *Smooth. That was real smooth Riley.*

"That's great." She gritted out, "Feel free to use them with Nanette."

"But I don't want her."

She humphed. The sound a clear, *yeah, right.*

He rubbed a hand through his hair and grunted. "I am not doing this well."

Di shook her head. "What is it you're doing?"

"I like you," Riley confessed. "I like you a lot."

"No, you don't," Di shot back. "I like beer."

"So do I." He took a step toward her.

She took a step back. "I wear cotton t-shirts."

With X-rated underwear underneath, but he didn't think that's what she was getting at. "So do I."

She took two steps back. "I don't have size triple D breasts."

Riley's gaze dropped to her chest. "Your breasts are perfect." He took two steps toward her.

"Oh." She flushed. "I'm not your type."

"I don't have a type."

"But—"

"Forget it. Yes I do. My type is *you.*"

He swore he could see her melt. But he wasn't finished so he kept going, "You have a compassion inside you that is beautiful. You want to help kids. You're incredibly book smart. I love that about you." Riley ticked off all the things he admired about her. "You have a passion for others. You have edges."

"I have edges!" she cried desperately.

"I love your edges," he said decisively.

"No, you don't."

"I do." Riley stepped into her personal space, so close they were almost touching. "I also love when those edges soften and sweeten, just for me."

"Oh, they do not." She propped her fists on her hips but she leaned into him.

He grinned. He couldn't help it. "Yes, they do." He brushed a stray curl off her cheek and stared into her pale, blue eyes. He demanded again, "Come home with me."

"You're crazy," she whispered.

"Crazy for you," he whispered back. He was crazy about her. He loved her smart mouth. Loved how she called him on his bull. Loved how she gave with her entire heart. Loved her. Which was crazy. He certainly couldn't confess that right this moment, she'd never believe him.

"Really, Stone?" But she didn't back away.

He shrugged. He couldn't completely turn it off. "It's true." And then he kissed her.

Riley wrapped his arms around her waist and pulled her into the shelter of his body. Di hesitated, her mouth tentative and her palms hovered inches from his chest.

He poured every bit of thanks into the kiss. Thankful she came into the office and hired GHR. Thankful Jack didn't agree and go to Jolo with her instead. Thankful for the universe for throwing them together and forcing her to spend time with him. Thankful for her calling him on his bullshit and yet not giving up on him.

Her lean angular body melted against his. Riley took two steps back, pulled her with him, until he rested on the edge of Jack's desk.

Di's hands slid up his chest, and over his shoulders as he spread his legs and pulled her tighter into the deep V. Her sex hit right at his fully-aroused cock. He'd been hard since she started arguing with him.

Riley scooted further back and knocked the blotter aside, which created a chain reaction and the picture and pen clattered to the floor.

With every fiber of his being he prayed that Jack had condoms in his desk. Riley pulled her closer, tighter, not wanting to give her any room to change her mind. She was his.

Di melted into Riley's embrace.

As if he wanted to anchor her to him, he pulled her closer and slid his hands over her ribs and cupped her breasts under his white t-shirt.

She arched into the erotic touch. Arousal flushed through her. Goosebumps prickled over her skin at his firm, knowing strokes. With each caress, he ignited a separate erogenous zone. Oh God. She couldn't resist this, him. She wanted him on top of her, inside her, she craved him like a drug.

"I want you," he confessed between drugging kisses. "Bad."

Oh thank goodness they were on the same page. But —"What about your rules?" No condoms.

Riley broke away from their embrace and circled the desk. "Pretty sure Jack has condoms in his desk." He yanked open the top drawer. He held up a foil package in triumph then tossed it on the desktop. Riley hastily headed back around to the front of the desk and Di.

"I'll be sure to get disgusted by that later." She ripped his shirt over his head, while he unsnapped her pants. Now that she'd committed to the idea, she wanted to move at lightning speed.

"Wait." Riley grabbed her hands and held them tight to stop her from touching him.

But she wasn't stopping now. Di grinned with glee. "We're not waiting."

"You're sure?"

"Hell, yes."

Riley let go of her hands and pulled her shirt over her head. His thumbs rubbed over her lace-covered breasts and he smiled when her nipples stood at attention. "God, you're pretty."

Di flushed and averted her gaze from his, taking a moment to savor his exquisite body. His stomach muscles rippled and his biceps flexed in the glow from the desk lamp. His stubble was two days old and dusted his jaw and upper lip with dark hair. The beard emphasized his stunning, clever lips as he smiled at her before he dove back in to torment her breasts.

Di's sex tingled and her knees weakened as he nipped a path down the middle of her breastbone. Riley's fingers were tight on her hips as he held her still for his sensual assault.

She worked at his zipper, taking time to caress the large bulge of his cock.

He groaned against her belly button as she finally pushed his cargo pants down enough to wrap her hand around his girth. She almost crumpled into a puddle of desire as he pulsed in her grip.

He was big. And thick. And primed.

A drop of pre-come glistened on the head of his cock and Di wanted fiercely to taste him. Before he could stop her, she leaned over and lapped delicately at the proof of his desire. Riley jerked involuntarily and she moaned and sucked the head into her mouth. He tasted good and felt even better.

"Let me go down on you," she begged.

He laughed softly. "While I love hearing that, it's got to wait." His fingers dipped inside her lace panties and curled against her dripping sex. "You're so wet."

With a slick move, he slid one thick finger into her silken channel, then two, priming her for his cock.

Di rocked her hips to the rhythm of his hand and continued to rub her thumb over the tip of his cock.

"Fuck me." He groaned and grabbed the condom.

"Yes, please."

He ripped open the package and rolled the latex over his erection.

She was pushing her pants down her thighs. Di made a sound of frustration, she still had her boots on and wouldn't be able to get her pants off fast.

"Fuck. I can't wait. Stand up and turn around," he commanded. Riley bent her over the massive desk and shoved her pants down to her knees.

Di whimpered as he spread her legs as wide as the restrictive clothing allowed. He rubbed her wetness over her sex, teasing her. "Now Riley."

Riley positioned himself behind her. She could feel the roughness of his hairy thighs against the back of hers and his cock head rubbed along her slit. Di tilted her hips back. Ready to beg again.

She needed him inside her, *now*.

As if he understood, Riley slid home. The head of his cock hit her cervix and the root spread her wide. His balls slammed against her engorged sex. He was everywhere, his fingers tight on her hips as he set a brutal pace, slamming in and out of her. Each thrust tormented her, filled her, overwhelmed her, until she hurtled into orgasm. Her vision dimmed, went white as she held onto the desk and held on for dear life as he thrust, once, twice, three times and then he came in hot hard jets, his cock pressing, expanding her walls until she thought she'd pass out.

Di's knees buckled and she would have collapsed against the desk if Riley wasn't holding her up. He bowed back against the power of his orgasm as he pulsed inside her.

Di's heart pounded hard from the most explosive orgasm of her life. It was a wonder she was still conscious.

He surrounded her, his arms tight around her waist and his legs bracketing hers.

As conscious thought returned, she knew it would be easy to just sink into the swirl of sexual completion and avoid any kind of strife. But Di knew they needed to address some things. And she knew he'd handle her need to talk about it right now, because Riley could handle anything thrown at him. It was one of the things she admired most about him.

"We need to talk."

Riley smiled against her spine. He was still slumped over her back, his heart pounding against her, his hands holding onto her as if he never wanted to let her go. He pressed light kisses along her vertebrae, still buried balls deep inside her.

They couldn't talk like this. Di wouldn't be able to concentrate. Plus she wanted to see his face while they talked. He prolonged the contact for another few minutes, until she wiggled her hips.

"Give me a minute." Finally Riley pulled out of her and disposed of the condom. Di pulled her pants up to her waist, grabbed the white t-shirt and covered up her body, then walked around the desk to drop into Jack's chair. Her heart was still pounding and her body still throbbed. There was no way she'd be able to stand for this discussion.

"Why were you the one to take me to Jolo?"

Riley raised a brow as he yanked up his pants. "That's what you want to talk about?"

Not really. "Yes."

Riley sat back down on the desktop, his body still very close to hers, his chest still bare and distracting.

"Jack knew that besides the fact that I have the most experience in country, I believe in what you're doing for those kids," Riley replied.

And that's when she knew. Riley was the *right* guy. The man who had similar interests, who felt passionately about making a difference, who would love her for who she was, and nothing else.

Now she just had to convince him of that. "Why didn't you take Nanette up on her offer?"

"I don't want Nanette." Riley narrowed his eyes, clearly annoyed. "I want *you*. I'd think that was pretty obvious since you were just bent over the desk and I was buried inside you."

"Careful, your charm is slipping." But she didn't care. She realized that Riley charmed everyone because that was how he got along. But he didn't charm her. He didn't need to.

"So?" Now his tone was almost belligerent. "It doesn't work on you anyway."

"I worked hard to resist you on the outside."

"You seem to be doing a bang up job of it," he said sulkily.

Di leaned forward and brushed a lock of hair from his suspicious eyes. "But I have a confession."

He perked up at that.

Di's heart pounded. This was scary. And life-altering. But if they were going to go on, they needed to begin in the right place. And she realized that he'd bared his soul, now it was her turn. She stood up. Re-energized. "I was so busy resisting your outside charms, that I fell for what's on the inside."

"Really?" He wrapped his arms around her waist, as if he knew that just confessing that made her want to bolt.

"Really." She smiled at him. Her perfect hero was Riley. Even though he wasn't perfect at all, just a charming man with his own set of issues. "You're perfect for me."

His arms tightened around her waist. Riley slanted his head and began to kiss her again.

She stopped him. "Or maybe it's just the sex," she teased.

"All part of my evil plan to stun you with such incredible sex that you'd be too sated to do anything but agree to come home with me." Riley grinned.

It had definitely worked. Not that she'd let him give him that satisfaction. "Hmm. Not sure it worked."

Riley laughed and lifted her into his arms. He turned and lay her over the desk and began all over again. "Well, I'll never give up. Let's try again."

Twenty minutes later, Di was sprawled over the top of Jack's desk. Riley was sprawled over top of her. His head rested on her breastbone, her heart thudded against his ear as he played with her ridiculously sensitive nipples and gave thanks for the fact that she'd said yes. And that Jack had condoms in his desk.

The lamp shade was cockeyed and they were both butt naked.

The outer door to the office banged open.

"Riley?" Con's deep voice called out from the outer office.

"Shit," Di whispered.

"Con. Wait a minute."

"Everything okay?"

Riley lowered his forehead to her neck, his shoulders shaking with mirth. "It's great. We just need a minute."

"We?" Con started laughing. "Are you desecrating Jack's desk?"

Riley heard what sounded like Ava shushing Con's laughter. And suddenly he remembered those papers on the floor.

"We'll be out in a few."

Di was shoving at his shoulders frantically trying to push him off her so she could get up. But the movement was doing pretty fabulous things to her sweet pert breasts. And Riley couldn't help himself. He bent to give each one a slow sensuous kiss and suckled her, rolling each taut nipple on his tongue. And Di's fists stopped beating on his shoulders as she arched her back and pulled him closer.

Screw it.

Con and Ava had to wait a lot longer than a minute.

THANK you for reading Heart of Stone. I hope you enjoyed Riley and Di's story. If you did enjoy this book, below are a few ways you can help a writer out!!

Good: Lend the book to a friend

Better: Recommend the book to your friends

Best: Leave a review at Amazon, BN, Goodreads, Kobo, iBooks, and GooglePlay...basically any place they sell eBooks. Every review helps my work get out to other readers and I cannot even express how much it means to me when you let people know you liked my work. Readers have so many choices nowadays and limited dollars to spend. It can be difficult to take a chance on a new author even if the premise sounds appealing. By reviewing books, you give other readers insight into the story world and help them make informed purchases.

Thank you, thank you, thank you for your support!!

P.S. Would you like to know when my next book is available? You can sign up for my new release email list/newsletter at Lisa's Confidants

RILEY'S RULES

1. Never have sex without a condom and another form of protection

2. Never be deliberately mean

3. Never have sex without a condom and another form of protection

4. Always have something positive to say

5. Never have sex without a condom and another form of protection

6. Always have your sibling's back

7. Never have sex without a condom and another form of protection

8. No sex with clients

9. Never have sex without a condom and another form of protection

10. Never do more than lightly flirt with co-workers

*B*liss Lee rubbed her damp palms over her navy blue, Federally-approved pantsuit, and forced herself not to pace the elegantly appointed CEO's office of Adams-Larson International and Associates, lovingly and humorously dubbed ALIAS by the employees. She was the 'Associates' part of the agency. Which was fine by her. She didn't want the responsibility of running the whole shebang. She'd rather concentrate on their special clients.

"Relax," Jillian Larson, her boss, friend, and co-chairman of Adams-Larsen directed and threw up hands. "He's just a guy."

But Jack Stone wasn't just a guy. He was *The Guy*. The one who got away, even though she'd initiated their break-up. The one who, despite her attempts to find another guy, ruined her for every other man she'd ever been intimate with. Except that had been their problem. Jack Stone didn't really know how to be intimate.

Sex, yes. Emotional intimacy, no.

He'd been excellent at the sex part. But he'd never bared his private self to her. Although she'd had her own issues

with being completely honest, she'd tried as much as she could. Her lack of honesty was more omission than lying. But her awkward half-attempts and Jack's inability had been too much strain for their young relationship. And once he'd joined the Navy, she'd been done.

Unfortunately, Bliss had never found another bond close to what she'd had with Jack, flaws and all. Even her ex-husband couldn't measure up to Jack Stone. And after a long two years of trying to make their marriage work, they had, less than amicably, decided to end it. Her ex-husband had accused her of hiding things. And she had been. Most of all she'd been hiding the fact that she was still in love with a man she'd kicked out years earlier.

Bliss's throat tightened. "Keep telling me that."

Jillian raised one exquisitely-groomed blond eyebrow and smirked. "Gladly." Her friend was perfectly put together in her signature pencil skirt in black and a fitted black jacket with a flirty peplum accent.

Bliss couldn't pull off that outfit in a million years. Jill looked sophisticated, sexy, and in charge. Bliss stuck to borderline masculine suits and darted white or blue broadcloth shirts.

The intercom crackled. "Your appointment has arrived," Marissa said pleasantly through the communication system.

Bliss's heart boomed in her chest, furious and nearly out-of-control.

Jill's hand wrapped around Bliss's wrist tightly, grounding her, reining her in. Bliss took a deep breath, gathered her scattered composure, and nodded. "Ready."

"Show him in," Jillian said calmly to Marissa.

The perfunctory knock was quick and then the door

swung open. Bliss forced herself to turn, braced for the impact of seeing Jack Stone again.

Jack strode into the office like he owned it. Dressed in khaki cargo pants and a black t-shirt, the cotton strained across his forty-six inch chest, his huge biceps tested the hem of his short sleeves. He had a canvas duffel slung over his shoulder and a multi-dial watch strapped to his solid, thick wrist.

He didn't falter when his gaze connected with hers, but she was pretty sure his shoulders tightened almost imperceptibly. They locked gazes, his ever-changing hazel eyes appeared almost pure green today and mesmerized her with their intensity.

The shock of his penetrating regard held her immobile. She damned her extreme visceral reaction as stunning emotions and images from years ago waterfalled through her brain; Joy, Jack laughing as he picked her up and swung her around like she was a kid; Love, Jack lying in bed, sheets tangled around his legs, his large chest bare, arm propped behind his head, eager smile on his face, as he waited impatiently for her to join him; Lust, Jack with water droplets running down his body and disappearing into the wrap of his towel, the bulge of his erection a sign of his passion; Pain, Jack's stunned expression when she told him goodbye; and finally despair, the stark, unrelenting ache that gripped her for weeks and months after he'd left.

Each image and the emotion behind the remembrance pierced her heart, until she was sure she must be bleeding out onto Jill's intricately woven, twenty-thousand-dollar Persian carpet.

Jack stopped in front of Jillian, dropped his duffel to the floor, and held out his solid, wide palm. "Jack Stone." His hands were big and scarred and tough, just like the rest of him. Those hands had caressed every inch of her body and brought her to heights of ecstasy that she hadn't climbed since he'd left.

He looked good. Damn him. Better than good, great. He had some new lines around his eyes, and his hair was a little longer. His face had matured, the softness of the young adult he'd been was now honed to a sharpness that only ramped up his attractiveness. A thin strip of hair was missing from his right eyebrow, a white scar creased the arch, and her heart stopped as she recognized that the missing strip was likely from a bullet graze.

He'd almost had his head blown off.

She swallowed down the fear that mushroomed through her. Based on the faded whiteness of the scar, the damage had happened a long time ago.

He'd filled out since she'd last seen him, and he'd already been big to begin with. His physical size had been comforting and engendered a feeling of safety and security for a girl who'd had far too much upheaval and violence in her early life.

Not that Jack knew anything about that, of course. She'd never told him about her childhood. She wasn't supposed to tell anyone. Ever.

Jillian introduced herself, then said, "This is my associate, Bliss Lee."

Jack nodded briefly at Bliss, but didn't offer his hand. Instead he propped his hand on his waist. "We've met."

We've met? *We've met?*

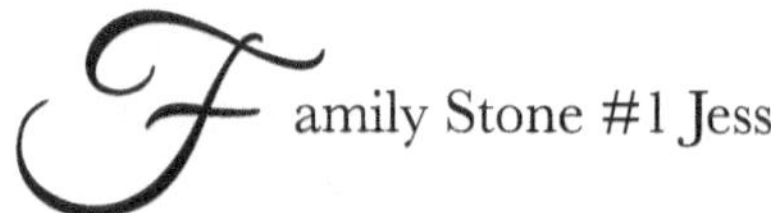amily Stone #1 Jess

IN THE EARLY EVENING DUSK, Jess Stone lay on her stomach in the twenty foot high rubble of a demolished church, underneath a black and gray city-scape tarp intended to camouflage her position. A sharp-edged chunk of debris dug into her lower rib cage, the scope of the Remington M24 cool and familiar against her face.

Her standard uniform of jeans, running shoes, and plain black t-shirt rendered her just another anonymous and transient relief worker...which she was actually. A black baseball cap hid her distinctive multi-hued blonde hair. The paper mask kept out the contaminated dust from the destroyed buildings but did little to stem the overwhelming stench of decaying bodies.

Tanks rumbled through the destroyed coastal town, their public address system blasting warnings for citizens to stay in their homes, curfew was in effect. The threat was a joke.

Ninety percent of the people in the town didn't have homes left. Those who did were terrified to go back inside. In the fetid, humidity choked air, the tent cities erected in the parks and on the beach were seething masses of the injured and shock struck.

The substandard construction in the small country had never been enough to withstand the angry might of Mother Nature. Buildings had toppled like a stack of Tinkertoys, and left crumbling cement walls with twisted rebar poking out of the jagged ruins like a skeletal hand.

Trapped in the concrete pieces that littered the ground, the heat from the tropical day seared through her thin sturdy clothing. The stank of the raw sewage that ran in rivulets through the streets overpowered the salt-laden breeze off the ocean. People, covered with the grit of pulverized buildings and humans, shuffled along with blank vacant stares. Two weeks after the quake, still in shock, their lives decimated first by nature and then kicked and beaten by the ineffectiveness of a flawed relief system. Hundreds of humanitarian agencies had descended on the population duplicating efforts and yet completely missing the need in other areas. The government was ostensibly trying to coordinate the effort, however the mass chaos was undeniable.

Through the Leupold Ultra M3 fixed power sight, she tracked the movements of Henri LeRoy, leader of this tiny island nation, violator of human rights and dignity, and all around poor excuse for a human being.

Sickness roiled in her stomach. The power bar she'd eaten for breakfast threatened to add to the rubble pile as she tried to figure out how in the hell she'd ended up here. Back behind a sniper rifle with the power over life and death trembling in the muscles of her right trigger finger.

Dammit. When she'd decided to take control of her life and quit the FBI, she hadn't wanted to do this any more.

She'd wanted to be a simple relief worker. She'd wanted to connect with her family, brothers and mother.

But that bitch, fate, had slapped her upside the head and now here she was, where she'd sworn she never wanted to be again. Looking through the scope of a high-powered rifle, with a crystal clear head shot and a murky sense of right and wrong.

With little fanfare, she could blast LeRoy's brain matter all over the silk-covered walls and the antique Louis the XIV scrolled chairs in the receiving room of his ridiculously elegant weekend mansion which, since built properly, had sustained minimal damage. Her muscles twitched with the knowledge and acceptance that with one slow slide of her finger, the despotic, amoral leader would be history.

Jess didn't want to kill him, didn't want to be directly responsible for another death. She didn't want this choice. She'd given up this kind of life. She'd left the FBI after a series of high stress cases to get away from the doubt and guilt that had crippled her. To make her own decisions about right and wrong rather than carry out the commands of her bosses.

But if Henri LeRoy lived, chances were astronomical that many other citizens would die.

And yeah, she'd probably been manipulated into this. Actually no probably about it. Assassination had not been listed as one of her duties when she'd joined Global Humanitarian Relief. Damn her brother anyway.

But now all she could do was lay here in the desecrated remains of the former church and hope that her special skill set wouldn't be needed.

Fortunately, she was secondary backup.

And unless several things went horribly wrong, she would break down her weapon, get back to the relief aid encampment, back to actually helping people, and be out of here without ever firing her rifle.

Then she could hand out seed packets to her heart's content and figure out what she was going to do next. If she'd stay with GHR and her brothers, or go. First, she had to get through the next two hours.

But if something did go wrong...she prayed that if she was called upon, she could make the right decision. Make the shot. Cold zero.

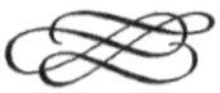

amily Stone #2, Connor

Ava Sanchez scurried toward her desk and cursed her tendency to blush. Luckily, with her swarthy skin tone and her current healthy tan—she'd spent a decent amount of time at the beach this summer—her blush likely wasn't *too* noticeable. However, she couldn't completely hide her deep embarrassment. When Jack had issued his 'no sex on the desk' command, she'd had no chance to temper her reaction. It was as if he'd reached right into her favorite fantasy and blurted it out to Connor.

She sighed. Connor, who never even noticed her.

Oh, he acknowledged her. He smiled. Said hello. But he never really *looked* at her. And maybe on the outside she appeared as a confident, well-dressed, well-groomed woman, but on the inside she was still that painfully shy wallflower, the migrant worker who didn't quite belong, who squeaked when spoken to and couldn't ever act normal in a social situation.

She'd worked hard to overcome her natural reticence. To learn to be polished and to strive for classy and sophisticated. To eradicate the dust and dirt from the fields and her native Sinaloan accent. She'd come a long way in the last eight years, but she still had difficulty speaking to men she found attractive. And she definitely found Connor Stone attractive.

"Sorry, Ava," Jack called from his office. She knew he was. He was gruff and a little rough around the edges but he meant well. He'd given her a job right out of college and helped her acclimate to a new world with affection and patience. He treated all his employees like family, which meant he frequently didn't think before he spoke.

Jack, she could handle. She grinned. "Expect my lawsuit in the mail," she quipped back, completely at ease with her totally hot boss. And he was. Totally hot. At thirty-four, he was also a little on the old side for her. But Ava wasn't attracted to Jack. He didn't make her girl parts tingle the way his brother did. Jack was like the older brother she'd never had and always wanted.

Jack gave a shout of laughter.

Why had Jack said that? Could he know that she frequently daydreamed about the youngest Stone brother? All the other women in the office were *loco* over Riley. And no doubt Riley was extremely handsome, smooth, and very charming. He always made her feel feminine and special. But he did that to everyone. Ava preferred the quiet confidence and the understated smarts of Connor Stone.

He was physically intimidating, as big as Jack and definitely as muscular. Since she wasn't a simpering skinny swizzle stick, but a solid woman with more curves than she'd like and the build of a peasant, Ava appreciated Connor's bulk. She imagined that he would make her feel delicate and dainty if he wrapped his solid, massive biceps around her and cupped her ass in his large palms.

"Hey." Connor stood in front of her desk.

Ava jerked and blinked up at him. She could feel an even deeper flush thunder through her body like a wave of heat. Great, while she'd been daydreaming, he'd been watching her imagine him naked and wrapped around her. "Er. Hello."

"Ignore him. He's an idiot."

"Okay. Thanks."

And if only he'd shut up then, because that was the perfect place to stop. Instead, he kept going. "Of course we aren't going to...."

Of course. Because no way could a guy that good looking, that smart, that *everything*, ever want to have sex with her. Ava's temper began to simmer. "Of course not." Her snide tone left no room for interpretation.

Connor looked very uncomfortable as he figured out that he'd just insulted her. "Uhhh, I don't think that came out the way I meant it."

And like that she boiled over. "How did you mean it?" she said sweetly, softly. She blinked at him with her most innocent, wide-eyed, non-threatening expression for the first time truly looking him in the eyes. He had gorgeous eyes, a sunburst of caramel, chocolate and a hint of pale green in a kaleidoscope of color. Tawny, gold, predatory.

He was a very smart man. And he'd figured out that no matter what he said, he was trapped and going to offend her. Like the very smart man he was, Connor backed away. "I meant no disrespect."

If that was the way he wanted to leave it. "Fine."

That stereotypical Latina temper was a stereotype for a reason but she usually left her hothead reactions at the door. She needed this job and most importantly, she wanted this job to atone for the past. It was a bonus that she loved working here. She loved that she was using her degree but also doing some good. GHR was the perfect vehicle for her need to do penance. For her luck in surviving when Maria...Maria hadn't.

"Ava...."

He wasn't going to go away until she forgave him for the insult and let him off the hook. Too bad she didn't want to forgive him.

"Sure. None taken," Ava said dismissively, clearly lying. She purposely stared down at her monitor and started typing away. Too bad she had no idea what document was open or what she was typing. If he looked at the screen, he would only see gibberish.

Connor stood in front of her desk, arms hanging limply at his sides, half-turned toward Jack's office, half-facing her, as if undecided about what to do next.

She continued to pretend that she was ultra-busy, praying he would go away so that she could run to the bathroom and compose herself. She could hear Jack on the phone in his office, arranging the company jet to be at the Monterey regional airport. Soon.

Jack didn't sound happy. And she wondered why he was doing his own scheduling rather than having her take care of it. There was plenty of work that he took care of himself already. But he always had her schedule their pilot, Shane, and make the travel arrangements.

Connor hadn't left the area by her desk and his presence was beginning to make her sweat. She wondered if Connor was going to use Jack's office while Jack was gone, and if so, how was she going to get any work done with him less than fifty feet away and always just...there? She'd be a distracted mess the entire time.

Out of the corner of her eye, she noted his feet had started moving.

Only he wasn't leaving. He was stalking toward her, literally like a leopard toward its prey. Finally, all she could see was his thick, muscular thighs and the intriguing bulge in his crotch, covered by tan cargo pants, before he slammed his hands down on her desk, his blunt fingers and wide palms flattened on top of the report she was supposed to be typing.

His biceps rippled as he leaned close, his broad solid torso loomed over her and Ava fought the urge to lean away from the clear menace in Connor's pose. "Let's get one thing perfectly straight," he said softly, his face was set in fierce lines, and his multi-colored eyes glowed with fiery intensity.

Ava hypnotically lifted her gaze to his face, overwhelmed by his sheer physical presence. Arousal tingled through her at his proximity and his obvious strength. "Just because I won't, doesn't mean I don't *want*."

Connor shoved up and off her desk, then strode purposefully away. Ava was struck speechless by his words as she watched the play of his glutes beneath his snug cargo pants. Her heart still beat erratically in her chest and either she'd had a major sugar crash from her hard boiled egg breakfast or all the blood in her head had rushed south to a very under-used body part.

One question kept circling in her suddenly light-headed brain: Did he just say he wanted *her*?

<u>Cold as Stone (John, Family Stone #7)</u>

<u>Family Stone Box Set (Stone Cold Heart, Carved in Stone, Heart of Stone, Still the One, & Jar of Hearts)</u>

<u>The Nostradamus Prophecies</u>

<u>View To A Kill #1</u>

Never Say Never #2

<u>ALIAS</u>

Stalked (ALIAS #1)

Hunted (ALIAS #2)

Vanished (ALIAS #3)

Deceived (ALIAS #4)

<u>Billionaire Breakfast Club</u>

His Semi-Charmed Life (Camp Firefly Falls #11 and Billionaire Breakfast Club #0)

Everything He Wants (Billionaire Breakfast Club #1 The Jock)

Queen of His Daydreams (Camp Firefly Falls #23 and Billionaire Breakfast Club #1.5)

ACKNOWLEDGMENTS

Thanks again to Adrienne Bell, LGC Smith, and Cecilia Gray for last-minute reads, unconditional support, and every single suggestion that made this book stronger. So glad you all loved Riley as much as I do and wanted him to be just right.

To LJ at Mayhem Cover Creations thank you, thank you for the beautiful covers!!

AUTHOR NOTE: TYPHOON HAIYAN

Author note: I wrote this story months before Typhoon Haiyan hit the Philippines. I debated adding in the disaster to the story but ultimately I chose to take literary liberty by pretending it didn't happen. However it did happen and millions of people were affected.

If you are interested in helping the people of the Philippines, Save the Children is doing wonderful work.

http://www.savethechildren.org/site/c.8rKLIXMGIpI4E/b.8856103/

Stone Cold Heart:

Jess Stone, former FBI sniper, always felt like the kid who looks in the candy store window but could never afford to go in. But on a humanitarian mission to aid an earthquake ravaged country, finally she finds a place where she fits, in Colin Davies' arms, and working for Global Humanitarian Relief, her big brother's company. But can the former SAS thaw Jess's stone cold heart?

Carved in Stone:

Connor Stone has always been odd man out in his family. Not the oldest, not the most charming, he'd had a lock on the youngest until another half-sibling came to live with them, so he raised hell in his youth. Con knows now the only way to redeem himself is with deeds, not words and sets out to prove once and for all he is worthy of the Stone family. When his older brother asks him to take care of business, Con finally will have redemption he craves. Except when Ava Sanchez, his brother's assistant, is threatened, he must choose between saving the girl or protecting his family. Will his choice bring him love or break his heart?

Heart of Stone:

Riley Stone is the handsome brother, the charming one. Everyone who meets him compares him to his father, which in his mind is not a compliment. But he's never met a woman he couldn't charm, until he meets Di, an acerbic, smart-mouthed, passionate activist who has no time for him or his charm. On the run, in the midst of danger, the blistering passion they share explodes. Can these two opposites find common ground, or will Di smash Riley's stone heart?

Still the One:

Jack Stone, former Navy SEAL, and oldest Stone sibling is determined to keep his family strong. Family is everything. So he starts Global Humanitarian Relief and Stone Consulting to do some good and keep his family together. But when he has to team up with his old flame, Bliss, on a missing persons case, an evil threatens him, his family and the one woman he could never forget and doesn't want to let go. Can these two former lovers put aside past hurts and heal their hearts?

USA Today Bestselling Author Lisa Hughey started writing romance in the fourth grade. That particular story involved a prince and an engagement. Now, she writes about strong heroines who are perfectly capable of rescuing themselves and the heroes who love both their strength and their vulnerability. She pens romances of all types—suspense, paranormal, and contemporary—but at their heart, all her books celebrate the power of love.

She lives in Cape Ann Massachusetts with her fabulously supportive husband, two out of three awesome mostly-grown kids, and one somewhat grumpy cat.

Beach walks, hiking, and traveling are her favorite ways to pass the time when she isn't plotting new ways to get her characters to fall in love.

Lisa loves to hear from readers and has tons of places you can connect with her. It's a wonder she gets any writing done at all....

Sign Up for Lisa's Confidants
Visit Lisa on the Web

Follow Lisa's Boards on Pinterest
Follow Lisa on Instagram
Email Lisa
Be Lisa's Friend on Goodreads
Like Lisa on Facebook at Lisa Hughey: My Books